FIERCE CYBORG

BOUND BY HER SERIES - BOOK 4

NELLIE C. LIND

Sense of Romance

High-level romance for romance lovers!

Fierce Cyborg
Bound by Her - Book 4
Copyright © Nellie C. Lind 2019
Cover and layout: Nellie C. Lind
Editing: Chrissy Szarek
Publisher: Sense of Romance
ISBN: 978-91-983128-1-2

PREFACE

Fifty years ago, the scientific and medical company, MedAct created the first male cyborgs. Their creator was the founder of MedAct, Carolyn Williams, and it gave every woman out there the opportunity to create the *perfect* man.

From the moment the cyborgs opened their eyes and became aware of the world, they were in love with the woman who'd designed them.

Society was told cyborgs couldn't exist without the bond to a human woman, and the cyborgs who survived the death of their bound one went crazy, or became dangerous. The only way to help them was to find a new bound one.

It was all a *lie.*

Celise Campbell, a MedAct doctor, learned it the hard way when her cyborg Wind almost died when his bond was being transferred to her from his previous bound one.

The bond was nothing more but poison, programmed to be released into the cyborg's system the moment their bound one died.

Sometimes, the poison failed to kill the cyborgs, and those who survived were the ones who knew the truth.

They became the Fighters, led by the first cyborg ever created; Nightmare.

Their goal; destroy the bond and set the cyborgs free.

The answer seems to lie in the secret female cyborg program.

CHAPTER 1

FORTY-TWO YEARS AGO

"You've been a bad boy, Zero. Do you really think you can get away with this?"

"Shut up," Zero hissed and pressed the gun harder against her temple. He squeezed his arm tighter around her chest.

It made her groan, but he tried not to care.

He was so close to freedom.

Several cars blocked both exits from the bridge. Their bright headlights illuminated the dark night, and the heavy rain slapped him in the face.

His long hair was glued to his cheeks and forehead, and every muscle ached from all the running.

Zero's shirt was drenched, and his bare feet, weren't used to the concrete. They were filled with blisters and wounds, making it agonizing to stand, but he forced himself to remain on his feet.

Despite him being more tolerant of the cold than humans, his body was shaking. It'd been hours since he'd been inside a warm and dry place.

At least fifteen guns were pointed at him by the men and women in black suits, but they kept their distance. They knew how strong he was. After all, he was created to be stronger than humans.

"Let me go." She wiggled to get free.

"Don't even try it, Carolyn. If I'm going to die today, I'm taking you with me."

"Oh, really?" She laughed, but the laughter was filled with ice. "Do you really believe you can kill me? Me, whom your heart loves so much?"

His grip on the gun tightened. It was true. He loved her, but not by choice. Some time ago, she'd done something to him, installed something within him. She called it "the bond," and it had made him fall in love with her, to such extent that he would die without her now.

Everything inside him protested against what he was doing.

Everything inside him told him to let go of the gun and give in, but he'd listened to those feelings before, only to end up badly beaten.

Never again.

Never again would he allow feelings to rule him.

No matter how much Zero wanted to cry out his desperation and need for the woman in his arms, he wouldn't give in.

He was her creation, but that was where it ended.

Carolyn would never have control over him again.

He'd find a way out as soon as his freedom was in his grasp.

Her fingers gently caressed his hands.

Zero cursed. "Stop that."

"Doesn't it feel good? Don't you want my touch?"

Oh, he did, but the humiliation that followed; he could live without. He'd lost count on how many times he'd shared her bed because of the bond. It gave him no other choice but to want her, no matter how everything else inside him screamed. "I won't let you destroy me the way you destroyed my brothers."

"They were weak, worthless, but you ..." She caressed him again. "You're my perfect creation."

He snorted. "You don't give a shit about me. You only use the bond to control me and to fulfill your sick sexual fantasies."

Carolyn turned her head toward him and grinned. "And you liked every minute of it."

Rage filled every part of him. He wanted to fire the gun, blow her brains out, and watch the bitch take her last breath. It would be a satisfying moment, but the bond stopped him.

The love for her sang inside his chest and almost made him embrace her instead. Having her body pressed against his was pure bliss, a sweet candy Zero never wanted to stop tasting, but he resisted the impulse. "Do you really want to find out how deep my hate for you goes?"

She tensed and her lips flattened to a thin line.

Good.

That meant she wasn't completely sure about the bond being the stronger emotion.

He could control her with that fear.

"Do it. Kill me", she hissed. "You'll be dead within seconds."

"I'm not afraid of death. I welcome it. Anything to get away from you."

The humans in black suits started to advance. Their guns still pointed straight at him.

Not good.

They wouldn't hurt Carolyn, but he was done for, no matter what he did. Giving in now was not the answer though.

He couldn't allow his brothers' sacrifices to be in vain.

He had to escape, because the world needed to know what was going on, but this might be the end of his road after all.

Zero frantically scanned the large bridge.

Surrounded.

He'd be dead soon, only a number in Carolyn's statistics, and she'd just start over, create others like him, and they'd be oblivious to what'd happened before them.

That filled him with sadness.

"There's no way to run, Zero. Give up."

Zero glared at the humans and slowly backed against the

railing. He didn't *want* to die. There *had* to be a solution.

The waves splashing against the foundation of the bridge caught his attention.

"Let me go, and I'll let you live," Carolyn said.

He snorted. "Do you take me for a fool? You'll only put me back in my chains and continue your painful experiments, and once you're done with that, you'll visit me at night to fuck me. All I am to you is a toy."

"Yes, my dear Zero," she chuckled, her voice filled with disgusting sweetness. "You *are* nothing more but a toy."

His anger rose to new levels. It exploded in his chest like a mad fire, and somehow, overpowered the bond, giving him that slim window where he could do whatever he wanted to her.

Zero squeezed Carolyn's arm hard, making her squeal and fight him, but she was weak compared to him, and right now, he didn't give a shit if he broke a bone or two.

He leaned closer to her ear. "My name's not Zero. It's Nightmare." He pushed her, and she hit the pavement with a groan.

Without giving Carolyn a second look, he jumped over the railing as bullets swished by him.

The dark and deep water hit his body hard, numbing him for a split second, but freedom was within his grasp, and Nightmare was going to take it.

CHAPTER 2

Jade Silva, the CEO of MedAct, sat at her desk, staring at the computer screen, where the image of a rotating cyborg showed.

He was attractive with big green eyes, a gentle smile, and a fit body. He was another woman's dream, everything she'd ever longed for, but Jade's mind was too split to focus on that dream.

She pushed a hand through her thick hair, as frustration grabbed her. Focusing on filling in the cyborg's details was almost impossible. Her fingers lingered over the keyboard, but no words came.

Jade sighed and stood. She needed a break. She approached the huge window. It was a beautiful and clear morning outside.

People hurried in different directions among the tall buildings and skyscrapers, but they all looked like dots from where she stood on the eighteenth floor.

Jade loved her job, but for a split second, she wished she could switch places with one of them.

Just for one second.

There was a knock on the door.

"Enter," Jade said without moving away from the window.

"You wanted to see me?" a woman asked as she entered.

She didn't need to turn around to know the voice belonged to Janice Walker, a MedAct doctor, and Soul's bound one. "Has Soul returned from the infirmary yet?"

"Yes, a few hours ago."

Jade finally whirled and glared at Janice. Her frustration spiked.

The blonde woman didn't flinch. Instead, her brown gaze was strong, almost challenging, but she didn't move.

Janice was anything but sweet and cute. She towered over Jade with her six feet, fit frame, and slightly masculine features. Her strong jawline was tense, and her thick eyebrows were furrowed.

"Then why don't I see him in here?" Jade asked. "It's been days since he and the others returned from the warehouse, and I need to know what happened."

"Soul got wounded during the fight."

"He should be fine by now."

Janice opened her mouth to answer, but closed it again, maybe changing her mind about what she was going to say. After all, the doctor knew there was no point in arguing.

"I'll tell him to come here."

"Good."

Jade faced the window again and watched the flying cars swish by as her colleague left the room.

She'd barely gotten any sleep these last few nights, but she was used to being tired. It came with the job.

This time, four cyborg soldiers had occupied her thoughts and kept her awake.

Soul and three other cyborg soldiers had been sent to the warehouse where MedAct stored medical and technical equipment to stop Nightmare and his gang from stealing things.

She'd expected Soul to finish the mission the usual way, by informing her how it'd gone, but instead, she'd been greeted with silence despite their return.

Learning later he'd been wounded had filled her with worry, but cyborg soldiers were strong. A lot stronger than regular cyborgs. They'd been created for combat.

They were the perfect warriors.

MedAct had been Jade's life for many years. Cyborgs had fascinated her even longer. As a child, she used to watch them on the streets, amazed by how humanlike they were.

Even then she'd wanted to dedicate her life to them. Now, as MedAct's CEO, she was responsible for everything that could go wrong, and lately, things were moving in that direction.

The Fighters were up to something new.

It wasn't a coincidence that her laptop had malfunctioned

in the presence of two previous Fighters when she'd visited Faye and Silver to sign the contract between them. Someone had, without a doubt, hacked it and gotten their hands on the codes to the warehouse, despite her strong defense programs.

Hunter had been there, but he'd erased all information about the Fighters some time ago. Therefore, it couldn't have been him.

Silver was the most likely source. It was difficult to be one hundred percent sure, but if he was the culprit, it was a mystery how he'd done it. Her defense systems against hacking and viruses *should* be bulletproof.

The door opened again.

"You called," a deep male voice said.

Jade looked straight into the eyes of an exhausted Soul. She studied him in silence. There was something new in his shining eyes, something she'd never seen before.

Anger.

She flinched. This usually calm giant actually radiated a pinch of anger. That was surprising, but it didn't matter. She approached him. "Report."

The cyborg soldier pressed his lips together and remained silent for too long. "As we suspected, they got their hands on the codes and broke into the warehouse. They got away with one tank and other smaller things. We caught some Fighters but ..." His clenched fists turned white. "Nightmare got shot."

Jade gasped and her breath got stuck in her throat.

Her heart almost stopped from hearing those three words. "What?"

"The cyborg soldier who did it has been removed from duty and punished according to the law."

"Who did it?" Her voice was cold, but chaos ruled within her.

"Cloud."

Every cell in her body wanted to explode in pure rage. How many times had she told the cyborg soldiers that Nightmare was not to be harmed?

She'd lost count by now, and yet, Cloud had shot him, but yelling at Soul wouldn't change a thing.

Punishing Cloud according to the law meant he wasn't allowed to carry a gun and participate in confrontations with the Fighters for one year.

That didn't sound painful, but to a cyborg soldier, it *was* painful. They'd been created to keep the cyborgs and the Fighters in check, and not being allowed to do what they were designed for was difficult for them to handle.

Either way, she'd have a long talk with Cloud, as soon as possible, to try to understand what'd gone through his mind. Worst-case-scenario, he'd never work for MedAct again, and would be sent to XenthAid, the place where all cyborgs who were unable to function in society went.

Nightmare.

He was hurt somewhere out there, and that didn't ease the ache. "Where was he shot?"

"The head."

Pain shot through her chest and all professionalism went out through the window. "The head? What the heck was Cloud thinking? Were you able to see what condition he was in?"

"No, but Cloud said it looked bad. Nightmare was unconscious when they carried him to the van."

A long chant of curses fell from Jade's mouth. "Unbelievable." She pulled a hand through her hair, pacing the room.

Soul's eyes narrowed. "Why do you care so much about him?"

She shot him a glare. "I care about all cyborgs. I want all of you to be well, even the Fighters. Besides, he's the first cyborg ever created."

Even if she was trying to help, she and Nightmare had been at each other's throats ever since she'd become MedAct's CEO, about fifteen years ago, and after Alexander Fleming's—the previous CEO—disappearance.

Despite Jade's efforts, Nightmare still wanted her dead, but she wanted him to live and be happy.

He'd find that happiness if he decided to bind himself to a woman again.

She'd told him so many times, but he didn't see it like that. Binding himself again was a death sentence to him.

Jade couldn't for the world understand why.

She, and everyone working at MedAct, knew so little about the Fighters. Trying to understand how they thought and functioned had been a long and difficult road, because the Fighters refused to co-operate. In their eyes, MedAct was the enemy.

All she and the other doctors knew was that there was something wrong with their bonds. The theory was that the Fighters survived their bound one's death because a small part of the bond remained intact. That small part kept them alive, but also made them unpredictable and dangerous, because the bond kept screaming for a new bound one—a new woman to belong to.

There was so much unknown, but at least one thing had been confirmed, thanks to the former Fighters, Silver and Hunter.

A simple kiss could initiate the bonding process.

No wonder the Fighters stayed away from women.

Soul watched her with worried eyes. The massive blond cyborg soldier didn't seem to know what to think about her outburst.

She rarely exploded, but this time, it'd been impossible to hold the anger in. She'd been on edge ever since she'd discovered her laptop had been hacked. Jade cleared her throat. "Was Celise there?"

He didn't answer at first, but his eyes twitched.

Jade frowned. Why was he hesitating?

"No," he answered after a while.

"Faye and Silver?"

He remained silent again. "It was dark and difficult to see."

Her frown deepened. "You're a cyborg soldier. You see

better in the dark than humans."

More silence greeted her.

"Not this time," he finally said.

Was he hiding something?

She had a hard time reading him, but her suspicion spiked. Jade *knew* Soul, they'd been friends for years, and he'd never behaved like this.

Something was wrong.

He seemed eager to leave her office, and that was unusual, too. As long as he didn't have another duty, he guarded her. Strangely enough, he preferred guard-duty over spending time with his bound one, Janice Walker. That was not normal for a cyborg, but Soul refused to tell her why.

Jade sighed. "What else?"

"We caught Heaven."

She gasped. "Where is he now?"

"On his way to XenthAid, along with the other Fighters we caught."

Jade clenched her fists. "Who ordered it?" Somehow, she managed to keep her voice calm.

"Amber Hill and Janice Walker."

She flinched. "What?"

Soul remained still, his expression, as if cut from stone.

How *dare* they?

Janice Walker and Amber Hill, the CEO of XenthAid, did this behind her back? They had *no* right to do as they pleased.

Written approval from her was needed before a cyborg

was sent to XenthAid. Heaven deserved a second chance, and so did the other Fighters that'd been caught.

Jade took two deep breaths to calm herself. "You may leave."

Soul was out of the room within two seconds.

Something was going on. She knew him well enough to know he wasn't telling her the complete story. Soul was usually open with her, but even if they were friends, he was a cyborg soldier first.

She picked up her cellphone but stilled when an image of an injured Nightmare crossed her mind. Jade imagined him lying on the ground, blood running from his head as he stared ahead with a dead gaze.

It made her hand tremble.

The bastard just had to go and get himself hurt.

Jade pushed the digital buttons on the phone and placed it against her ear as it connected. Her hand refused to stop shaking. The phone beeped in her ear.

"Hello?" a female voice asked.

She tried to relax and smile. "Celise. Hi. It's Jade Silva. How're you doing?"

"Thank you, I'm fine. To what do I owe this pleasure?"

Was that tension she heard in Celise's voice?

"Can you meet me tomorrow? I have something important to talk to you about."

"Sure. What do you want to talk about?"

The doctor sounded way too self-assured. Where had her normal shyness gone?

"Um …" Jade had to come up with something quickly. "About your continuing education. You're doing a great job in Glaswell with all the cyborgs, and I was thinking about recommending you for the Construction Program. I know you've always wanted to work with the process. Therefore, I think it's time."

It wasn't a lie. Celise was more than ready, and it was also the perfect excuse to meet with her. If her employee had anything to do with the previous day's events, Jade had to find out.

The doctor gasped. "Really? Oh, my God! Thank you! I'll gladly meet with you tomorrow."

At least her joy sounded real.

"Good. I'll stop by your and Wind's house at noon."

"Great! See you then."

Jade ended the call, slowly lowering the phone from her ear. She remained still, staring at the device.

She had to plan this well.

CHAPTER 3

Jade pulled into Celise's and Wind's driveway. She got out and looked up at the impressive blue two-story house.

Wind and his late bound one, Diane, had decorated the exterior with beautiful flowers by the windows and white curtains on the inside, giving the home an elegant and fresh look.

The garden was a colorful masterpiece, with a statue of an angel in the middle and white gravel on the ground, but the house and garden weren't important.

Finding out if Celise had anything to do with the events at the warehouse was her mission.

The only way for the Fighters to get access to the warehouse was if a MedAct doctor had let them in.

Jade hoped she was wrong, but Celise was the only option that made sense. After all, she was responsible for Silver, and even if he was bound to Faye now, Jade didn't trust him.

She knocked on the door.

A short moment later it opened, and the cyborg Wind greeted her with silence and emotionless eyes. Celise's cyborg was dressed in jeans and a white T-shirt, and the usual scent of paint wasn't on him. His long brown hair was tied in a ponytail. He, who usually was a calm and gentle cyborg, now radiated a pinch of anger.

She gave him a stiff smile. "Hello, Wind. I'm here to talk to Celise."

"I know." He didn't move away from the door. Instead, his eyes narrowed.

The way he looked at her sent a cold chill down Jade's spine. He'd never looked at her like that before. Where had the coldness and the anger come from?

Wind seemed to be judging her. Could it be that he still blamed her for not telling him about the pain he had to go through when he switched his bound one?

"May I enter?" she asked.

He finally let her in, but his eyes never left her.

Jade stepped inside a huge wide hallway. A scene of beauty and bright colors greeted her.

A chandelier hung from the ceiling, a beige carpet lay in front of the staircase that led to the second floor, and every wall was filled with beautiful landscape paintings Wind and Diane had created.

Her lips twitch. The house was amazing, and a pinch of envy filled her. She had an apartment on the top floor of the MedAct building. Sure, her place was huge and elegant, but nothing compared to this house. Jade noticed movement in the corner of her eye.

A smiling Celise entered the hallway from the living room. "Welcome. I'm glad to see you."

"Thank you." She gave the same stiff smile she'd had for Wind. Acting wasn't her thing. Jade could only hope her fake smile would cover her real reasons for being there. Reasons that had little to do with Celise's continuing education.

Finding clues would, without a doubt, be difficult. Her friend would never tell her straight out she'd been the one to give the Fighters access to the warehouse.

Hopefully, Jade's suspicions were wrong.

Celise was too kind, too gentle, to be the culprit, but on the other hand, there was a strength in the doctor she'd never seen before.

"I know why you're here," Celise said.

She blinked. "You do? I mean, of course, you do. We spoke about it over the phone yesterday … the Construction Program."

Her colleague nodded, her smile turned forced. "Of course, the Construction Program." There was a pinch of sadness in her voice.

Warning signals went off in Jade's head. That reaction wasn't the expected one.

Wind shut the door, and when the sound of him locking it filled Jade's ears, cold chills traveled down her spine again.

Was there a tension in the house? Or was she simply overreacting and imagining things?

She swallowed. Maybe she shouldn't have come alone. She should've brought Soul, just in case.

No, not Soul. Another cyborg soldier would've been better. Like Rain or Dare. Something wasn't right with Soul right now; something that made her wary.

Celise pointed toward the living room. "Let's sit down and talk."

Jade glanced at the closed door.

Wind headed for the living room, leaving her way out open.

All she had to do was take a few steps, unlock the door, and leave, but then she'd never find out about Celise's involvement. A few indications that something was off was all she needed. It would be enough for her to dig deeper.

Much pointed to Celise's guilt. She'd been there when Jade's laptop had been hacked, and she was also the only MedAct doctor who'd spent time around Silver and Hunter.

Sure, there were other MedAct doctors in Glaswell, doing the same thing as Celise, taking care of the cyborgs, but none of *them* had anything to do with Silver and Hunter.

Was it a coincidence that the Fighters had broken into the warehouse just a few days after her laptop was hacked?

Not likely.

Jade clenched her fists.

She could do this. She had to.

She had to find out why the Fighters had stolen a tank from the warehouse. Tanks were only used to create and heal cyborgs, so the reason was obvious, but were they really planning to create a cyborg?

Nightmare hadn't been wounded until after the tank was stolen. To her understanding, and the other cyborg soldiers' reports, the tank had already been in the Fighters van when he got shot, so it couldn't mean it was intended for *his* healing.

Did they have the knowledge to create a cyborg? She doubted it. A cyborg couldn't be put together from just reading a few books; it was way more complicated.

And Celise wasn't qualified.

So why? *Why* had they taken the tank?

It didn't make sense.

She scanned the living room. Running away wasn't the answer. Jade had to find out what was going on.

If Celise really *was* involved, it could, and would, damage MedAct.

Determination filled her. She took a deep breath and followed her colleague.

The room was a wide and open area, filled with elegant wooden furniture. Only the table Wind had ruined the day Celise became his bound one was gone.

No wonder. He'd squeezed one leg into pieces as the pain the bond caused him had surged through him.

A tiny pinch of guilt filled her.

Maybe she should've told him about the pain.

Jade inhaled and straightened her back. No, telling him would've made him back out.

All cyborgs who'd been told had changed their minds.

24

She froze when her gaze found the cyborg that sat on the sofa.

Silver.

The blond and attractive cyborg gave her a wide grin as he stood. "Welcome. We've been waiting for you."

Faye, his bound one, entered the room through another door with a tray in her hands. It was filled with tasty-looking sweets. She grinned at Jade, too. "Cookies? I've made them myself." She placed them on the table in front of her cyborg.

Silver pushed the plate away.

"Hey! What are you doing?" Faye glared.

"Spare yourself a cough attack," he told Jade. "She added too much salt. I almost threw up."

Faye's chin dropped. "Why, you … You told me you liked them!"

He grabbed her and pulled her to him. "Of course I did. It made you happy, and that's what matters." He pressed his lips to hers.

Faye giggled, her anger washed away.

Jade blinked. "What're you doing here?"

"Don't worry," Celise said. "I'll explain everything."

She narrowed her eyes. Her suspicion rose to new levels. "Right. I think I'll leave now. We'll talk about your education some other time." She retreated, ready to flee.

The warning signals sang louder in her head.

Jade jerked to a halt when something hard and cold touched her back. Slowly, she whirled, with a lump in her throat … and stared into the eyes of an angry Soul.

He aimed a gun straight at her. "I insist." His voice was cold.

Disbelief filled every part of her, but the frigidness in his eyes said he meant business.

"What the hell are you doing?" Obviously, Jade hadn't been wrong about him.

"Pat her down," Soul said, ignoring her question.

Silver approached. "Now, be a good MedAct CEO and spread your legs and arms." Amusement sparkled in his shining eyes.

She cursed on the inside, but obeyed. She was small compared to him, and her strong personality wouldn't help her. Besides, there were three cyborgs in the room, and one of them was a soldier. She glared at Soul. "I never expected this from you."

He didn't answer, but his anger was unmistakable.

Silver patted her down, and the strength in his hands was frightening. He could break her bones without much fuss if he wanted.

"If you hurt me, you'll regret it."

A short burst of laughter left his mouth, and he invaded Jade's personal space, towering over her. "Show me how exactly."

She swallowed but didn't say anything. Slapping him was tempting, though.

Silver grabbed a chair. "Sit."

She straightened her back. "I'll stand."

He sighed and forced her down on the chair.

"You—" she hissed between her teeth.

Silver was instantly in her face again. "I what?"

Jade didn't say anything more, but he made it more and more difficult to fight the urge to slap him.

"Just as I thought." He snorted, then ripped the bag from her hands.

Jade winced. "Hey! Give that back."

The former Fighter ignored her and rumbled through her belongings, examining every electrical device, and making a complete mess. When he was done, he threw the bag to her and turned to the others. "She's clean."

Celise frowned. "Nothing at all?"

"Nope," Silver said. "I'm just as surprised."

Jade remained silent.

They didn't need to know that she never carried any tracking devices. She hadn't given it a thought this morning, because, she hadn't expected to be captive.

Jade's mission was only supposed to include a conversation and gleaning information she needed.

No, she hadn't seen this coming, but now she knew.

Celise *was* the doctor who'd let the Fighters into the warehouse.

Jade crossed her arms over her chest and glared at Celise. "I guess this means you won't be going back to school any time soon."

The sadness that came over the doctor was impossible to miss. "That future is out of my reach now."

"Well, I'm not feeling sorry for you one bit, but you

better have a good explanation for all this." She looked around the room.

Silver was back at Faye's side on the couch.

Wind stayed close to Celise. His unusually chilled gaze was still there.

Soul blocked the way out. The gun was still in his hand and his gaze was fixed on her.

When he'd gotten involved wasn't difficult to figure out, but *why* and *how*, were two more complicated questions. Besides, how could he be here without Janice's approval? Was she in on it, too?

As a cyborg soldier, he was unable to go against an order his bound one gave him; it didn't matter if he liked the order or not. "Did Janice tell you to come here?" she asked Soul.

His gaze darkened. "No."

Jade frowned. "Then how—"

"Nothing you need to care about," he barked.

"Soul's here because he wants to be," Celise said, "but we're not here to talk about him. We're here because we need your help."

Jade couldn't help but laugh. This situation was becoming more and more surreal. "You expect *me* to help *you*? You must be out of your mind. First, you've obviously sided with the Fighters, and now, you want me to help you? Why did you let them in, Celise? And why on earth did you take a tank from the warehouse? You don't have enough knowledge to create a cyborg. It's way too complicated."

Her colleague didn't move. Didn't say anything either,

but her eyes spoke plenty. There was a story in them. A story she seemed eager to share, but her lips were sealed. "Nightmare's hurt," Celise said finally.

Jade couldn't breathe for a few seconds. Even if she'd already known, it still hurt like hell. "How badly?"

"The wound has healed, but he's not waking up. The damage is in his program."

She frowned. "Is that why you stole the tank, to try to reprogram him?"

Another silence fell. No one spoke.

Jade sighed. "Look, if you want me to help, you need to bring him to MedAct." She rose from the chair. "Call me when you're ready to do that." She turned around, hoping they would let her go, but when Soul pointed the gun at her again, she clenched her fists. "Do you think killing me is going to help you?"

"No one's going to hurt you," Celise said, "but you're not allowed to leave."

Holding in the anger that boiled in her veins was becoming more and more difficult. "Let me guess. You intend to tie me up, blind me, and drag me away somewhere so you can force me to save Nightmare. Am I right?"

Silver chuckled. "Something like that, but it will be easier to just drug you."

"Do you honestly think kidnapping me will go by unnoticed? If I don't go to work tomorrow, the cyborg soldiers will instantly start searching for me."

Silver only laughed more. "Let us worry about that."

Something sharp hit her in the arm, making her jerk and wince from pain. Jade grabbed it and pulled it out.

A dart.

Another wave of disbelief filled her as she met Soul's gaze.

The cyborg soldier stood in front of her with that gun still pointed directly at her.

He'd fired it.

"I can't believe you shot me. I thought we were friends."

He grabbed her as Jade's knees gave out. His face was hard as stone. "We were."

Darkness took her.

CHAPTER 4

Jade groaned and opened her eyes. Her eyelids were heavy and her sight was grainy, as if she'd been asleep for a long time. The fog in her head was stubborn and the dizziness uncomfortable, but slowly, both started to clear.

Whatever Soul had drugged her with was leaving her system. Thank God she didn't feel sick. Throwing up was the last thing she needed.

Betrayal sang in her heart. She'd never in a million years believed Soul would turn on her. They were friends, for heaven's sake!

Why had he done it? *What* was she missing?

Sure, things weren't right between him and Janice, but he'd never wanted to talk about it, so she'd dismissed it.

It was rare that a relationship between a cyborg and his bound one didn't work. Honestly, it was almost unheard of.

Maybe she saw something that simply wasn't there, but

something *had* made the cyborg soldier betray her and everyone at MedAct.

Something *had* happened at the warehouse.

That much she understood.

Jade blinked and looked around. She was inside a small but fresh room with white walls. There were no windows. There was only the bed she lay on and a toilet. A curtain could be pulled around it. The place had a claustrophobic feeling. Thankfully, she had no such issues, but the tension in her body grew.

Was she inside a prison?

Being around newborn cyborgs on a daily basis sure put things on perspective because of their overprotective nature. Tension and fear were common feelings, but *this* was something completely different.

She took a deep breath, not allowing the fear to set, but it was difficult. She had no idea where she was and no idea what awaited.

Trusting Celise's word that she wouldn't be harmed, was hard. She doubted they'd hurt her as long as they needed her to save Nightmare, but after that?

Who knew.

A rush of worry filled her. What if Nightmare was beyond saving? What if, not even *she* could save him?

Jade bit down, holding back tears. That idea was the last thing she needed right now. She didn't know the details, but she'd never forgive the Fighters, if it turned out to be too late.

The ache in her heart grew.

Nightmare had threatened her life plenty of times, but all she wanted was for him to abandon his pointless running around as a Fighter and come back home to the other cyborgs and MedAct.

Every cyborg needed MedAct and a bound one. There was no other way for them to be complete.

The Fighters agenda was unknown, because she and the other doctors didn't force information out of them. That wasn't MedAct's way.

Instead, Jade wanted the Fighters to understand they had nothing to fear, but no Fighter had ever trusted her with that reassurance.

They'd all laughed instead.

That didn't make sense.

Why did most cyborgs turn their backs on MedAct after their bound one's death? Those who returned never looked at the doctors and the scientists the same way ever again.

Did they know something she didn't?

The door jerked open, and she winced.

She stared at the red-haired cyborg who'd entered. He was attractive, fit, and tall, but his shining eyes glared with hatred.

Blaze.

Jade whole body went stiff. She'd never met him, but she'd heard of him. Even if she hadn't known his name, the hint of red in his eyes gave him away. He was the only cyborg with those type of eyes.

His anger wasn't personal, but keeping her distance would be wise. The anger was directed at MedAct, and as the CEO, *she* was his main target right now, because Blaze was convinced MedAct killed his bound one a few years ago.

She'd investigated his claims several times without ever finding any proof, but his feelings for the company were well known by all the doctors and scientists—like all the Fighters.

"Doctor Jade Silva," he said. "We finally meet. I can't say I'm happy to see you, but since there's no other way, your presence is necessary. I assume you know who I am."

She nodded. "Blaze."

"And you've heard my story." It wasn't a question.

"Yes."

"Good. Then you know to keep your distance."

She didn't flinch. She wouldn't be intimidated by him.

Jade worked with cyborgs and knew how to handle them. Besides, she was familiar with many of the Fighters. Their names, their stories, even their serial numbers. Some, she'd even created. They were nothing new, nothing to be surprised by.

Celise entered. Her expression was stern and distant.

It was the same expression every Fighter had when they encountered someone from MedAct. The disappointment in the doctor's eyes was unmistakable, but why?

Wind was just behind her.

"How are you feeling?" Celise asked.

"I'll live."

For how long, only they knew.

"I must say, I expected it to be more difficult to kidnap you."

Jade snorted. "It's the consequences you should worry about."

A few breaths passed before she answered. "We knew what we were doing."

"Really? Then please explain, because I have no idea what's going on."

"We need your help to save Nightmare."

She glared. Her heart clenched from hearing his name, and she tried to ignore it. "You mentioned that, but you're not answering my question."

"You haven't asked one."

Jade clenched her fists. "Why are *you* here? Why on earth are *you* working with the Fighters? When did that happen? You were one of my best doctors, and this is how you repay me?"

The sternness in Celise's eyes melded into anger. "You know very well why I'm here, *why* I joined them."

Frustration washed over her. "No, honestly, I don't."

"You lied to me. You lied to all of us. MedAct is fake. You *know* why the Fighters hate you more than anything. They learned the truth about the bond when they survived their bound one's deaths."

Silence filled the room.

Jade stared, and for a long moment, didn't move. Instead, she tried to grasp what her colleague had just said. "You sound like one of the Fighters. What did they brainwash you with?"

Celise stomped her foot. "Don't lie to me!"

She jerked back. "What the heck happened to you?"

The younger woman frowned. "You know what the bond *really* is."

Had Wind's bound one gone crazy?

"The bond is a program that the cyborgs need to live. They can't function without it, and when their bound one dies, the bond collapses, which kills the cyborgs. The Fighters live because a small part of the bond survives. There's nothing else. Never was, never will be. You know this."

Another silence filled the room, and the air thickened.

Wind, Celise, and Blaze exchanged gazes.

Confusion and anger radiated in their eyes.

Disbelief as well.

"How can you be so sure?" Blaze asked. "You barely know *anything* about us. You just recently learned an intimate touch can initiate the bond. Until then, you knew nothing."

How did he know that? Maybe Celise had told him.

"Because there can't be any other explanation."

Blaze's mouth pulled down at the corners. "So, you're saying you have no idea what happens with the bond when our bound one dies?"

Jade blinked. Hadn't she just explained that?

The surrealness grew by the minute. Sure, she could tell him more about how the bond collapsed, but that wasn't what he was after.

He wanted to hear something else, but what?

"You're all out of your minds."

Blaze sighed. "Enough." He grabbed her arm and pulled her to her feet. "We don't have time for this."

She didn't get the chance to respond.

He dragged her out of the room and into a long and white hallway. It was well lit, and with doors on each side every few feet. Was she in a hospital?

"What is this place?"

"The less you know, the better," Blaze said.

Jade was led into a huge space filled with computers, pool games, and other entertainments, but what filled her with dread wasn't the room itself.

It was all the Fighters there, all with their furious gazes set on *her*.

She'd never felt this small before.

Jade recognized several of them, and when one stopped in front of her and Blaze, she almost squeaked.

Thankfully, she managed to keep it together and not make a complete fool out of herself by following her instincts and run.

The Fighter didn't say anything, but he scowled with his big and shining eyes. He was tall, with the body of a dancer and an androgyny-like appearance.

His copper-red hair was combed backward and styled. The only thing that interfered with his slightly feminine beauty was his strong jawline and strict lips.

Phoenix.

"You're alone. No one wants you here," he said. "I'm the only one who has some patience with you, because you saved my life many years ago. Remember that."

She gave him a stiff smile. "It's nice to see you, too."

Blaze pushed her. "Nightmare's waiting."

They entered another white hallway and followed it before stopping in front of two double doors.

Jade swallowed for what felt like the hundredth time. Was Nightmare on the other side of those doors?

She barely dared to imagine what she'd see, but an image of him lying on a bed with pale skin, attached to tons of different machines danced into her mind.

Tremors chased each other down her spine. What if there was nothing she could do for him?

What if it *was* too late?

Blaze pushed a button next to the doors, and they opened.

She inhaled, unable to ignore how her heart thundered, but she followed him inside, expecting the worst.

CHAPTER 5

The doors closed behind them, after they entered the room.

Jade looked around. It was an infirmary; bright, clean, and filled with everything a doctor could possibly need to help someone.

There were beds, cabinets with drugs and medical equipment; all kinds of machines, but also cabinets with towels and clothing.

Apart from the beeping of a machine, the room was quiet.

Her heart cantered, and when she spotted the still figure on one of the beds, it clenched, then stuttered before beating again. For a split second, she forgot to breathe.

The machine was next to his bed. Lines and wires went into his body. It monitored his pulse and blood pressure, but also his cybernetics. The screen displayed that everything was fine there.

Her feet moved on their own. Slowly, she approached the bed.

Nightmare's eyes were closed, and his handsome features were calm. It was an unusual sight.

Jade was so used to seeing him angry, it was almost shocking to see him unmoving. Even the dark and hostile aura that usually surrounded him wasn't there. Not even the scar on his throat managed to amplify the dangerous vibes he always radiated.

Nightmare looked like any other cyborg about to wake up and start his life with his bound one.

His long hair lay beautifully around his head, but part of his black locks were covered with bandages. His shirt was open a slit, and the slight reveal of his fit and muscular chest awakened butterflies in her stomach. If that wasn't enough, the sight made her sex clench from desire.

Jade pressed her lips together. How she hated him for awakening this need every time they met, but she couldn't help it. It just came over her, making it almost impossible to pull her gaze away from the masculine attraction that he was.

She placed her hand on his arm. The feeling of his warm skin against her palm calmed her.

Thank God he was still alive.

Blaze and Celise stepped up the other side of the bed, and both studied her with narrowed eyes.

Jade pulled her hand away. "He seems well taken care of," she blurted. "What do you want me to do?" Her breath stuttered. Being this close to him, without him cursing at her or threatening her life, was almost thrilling.

She could stay by his side, hold his hand, and just allow the silence between them linger like a comforting blanket.

If she could get just *one* moment like that, *just one*, she could live on it for the rest of her life.

"He's not waking, even if he's healed," Celise said. "There's something wrong with his program, and we can't fix it, but *you* can."

"I see." That was all she could muster, but on the inside, the calmness she'd felt for a split-second, washed away.

How could they have allowed him to get hurt?

Why hadn't they stopped him from going? Hadn't he understood how dangerous it would be?

What an idiot!

Jade took a deep breath to stop from screaming out her anger.

Blaze, Celise, and the others still watched her.

Soul wasn't there though. Where he was, she didn't know, and she didn't care. He wasn't a friend of hers anymore.

"Do you have the data?"

Celise handed her a tablet. "I'm unable to decipher most of it."

She scrolled through the code, and gasped. With each number, each page, her hands trembled even more.

No one said anything, but no doubt, they noticed. They'd to be idiots not to notice how much her hands shook.

Jade almost dropped the damn device.

Nightmare's body was fine, thank God, but the chip inside his head containing his program was a complete mess.

It was beyond repair. He needed a new one, and he needed it fast.

The old one had to be removed.

Now.

... Or he'd die.

Honestly, it was a miracle he was still alive. It'd been days since he'd been shot.

"Is the tank operational?" she asked.

"No, why?" Blaze asked.

"He needs brain surgery and to be put inside the tank directly after." It was hard to keep her voice calm. The anger boiling in her veins wanted to explode. "The artificial chip inside his head is destroyed. Without it, he'll never wake up. It needs to be replaced and reprogrammed."

The medic cyborg's gaze hardened. "We'll do as you say, but if you try to kill him, *you* won't last long."

Jade shot him a glare. "I'd rather kill myself than let him die."

The Fighter winced and his eyes went wide. Shock was all over his expression.

The same astonishment reverberated among everyone else, too.

Damn.

She'd said too much.

"Please tell me you have all the necessary components to create a cyborg," she said, trying to ignore the awkward silence that'd fallen over the room. "I'm sure you stole some from the warehouse."

Blaze nodded. "What do you need?"

"I need a S.T.E.L-A chip, model fifty-one. It's ten times smaller than a fingernail and thinner than paper. We keep them in vacuum-sealed silver boxes. It should be easy to find."

Everyone in the room started to move, but Jade remained still.

Her gaze returned to Nightmare. She placed her hand on his arm again, and this time, she didn't care about the side-look Celise shot her.

CHAPTER 6

Jade couldn't remember the last time she'd been this exhausted. Her body ached from the long hours on her feet, and she wanted nothing more but sleep.

When she looked at the tank displaying Nightmare's sleeping figure through the glass, she straightened her back.

He needed her.

She couldn't go to sleep yet.

The surgery had gone well.

Celise and Blaze had been by her side. She'd taught them how to replace the chip, but she'd been the one to perform the procedure, since neither of them had the training.

Her colleague had devoured the knowledge like a sponge. It'd made Jade's lips twitch. Even if Celise was on the Fighters side now, her eagerness and desire to learn how to create cyborgs was still there.

Thankfully, they'd taken good care of Nightmare before

she'd come into the picture. They'd successfully removed the bullet from his head, and the wound had healed without issues, but the artificial components were on a completely different level.

Removing a bullet and replacing a damaged chip was like night and day, but thanks to their fast actions, Nightmare was still alive.

The worst was over. Now, he needed time to heal.

The Fighter's leader had been given drugs to speed up the healing process. A wound that usually took weeks for a human to heal would heal within a day or two for a cyborg. The tank also sped up the healing process even further.

She'd helped Celise and the Fighters to get it up and running. Without it, things would've been more complicated, but at least he was inside it now.

His condition was stable, and the new chip was one hundred percent operational and functioning as it should.

Even Faye and Silver had been by the operating table, but they'd just watched.

At first, it'd annoyed Jade. Usually, she didn't allow unnecessary personnel in the room during surgery, but she'd kept her mouth shut. After all, this wasn't *her* operating room.

Faye had observed everything.

Celise was obviously teaching her, and Silver had been there to protect Faye. From what, she had no idea.

Had he expected *her* to hurt his precious bound one? Jade snorted—then and now. Who did he take her for? She was surrounded by Fighters. What could she possibly do?

Stupid Fighter, but at the same time, she couldn't blame him for being overprotective. Every cyborg wanted to protect his bound one.

The infirmary was quiet.

Only Celise and Blaze were there.

They were doing something in the background, but Jade didn't know what.

She heard them mumble but couldn't tell what they were saying. It was obvious they didn't want her involved. They didn't trust her, and that hurt.

She took a deep breath and tried not to think too much about the future, but it was hard.

She'd saved Nightmare's life, but now what?

Would they get rid of her?

Jade studied him through the glass again. At least he was alive.

The leader of the Fighters would barely have a scar once everything was healed. New hair would grow out on the small area she'd to shave. The signs from the wound would almost be invisible.

Her gaze lowered to his throat. She had no idea how he'd gotten the ugly scar there. It must've happened a long time ago, long before she'd come into the picture, but it hadn't healed well, and was now a long and uneven piece of bulging scar tissue.

It was obvious no one had helped him with it. Nightmare must've been on his own when it'd happened.

Her heart tripped, and she couldn't help but see an image of a wounded Nightmare, sitting against a dirty wall somewhere, holding his hand against his throat as blood ran down his fingers.

He'd been on his own.

Alone.

How he must've suffered.

A tear ran down her cheek, but she quickly dried it away.

"Why are you crying?"

Jade winced when she heard Celise's voice behind her. She wiped away a second tear. "Don't worry about it. It's just pressure."

Her fellow doctor grabbed a chair and sat next to her. There was a pinch of pity in her eyes, but also understanding, and the gentle smile on her lips was, in a way, soothing. "You love him, don't you?"

She froze.

Time itself stopped for a split-second as her heart went into a frenzy. She held her breath, ready to deny it, ready to tell Celise she was stupid for even thinking such things.

Jade was ready for a fight.

Yet, she didn't move.

She stared at the tank, letting the question sink in, and after a long moment of silence, she nodded with a sigh. "Is it that obvious?"

Celise nodded. "Yes."

Jade pursed her lips. "Don't you *dare* tell him."

"I wasn't planning to, but someone else might."

"He won't believe it. It'll sound too surreal to him."

Was she trying to convince herself?

"How come you're so sure?"

"Because I'm Jade Silva, the CEO of MedAct. Besides, he and I have been on each other's throats since day one. He's never seen me as anything but someone he can't wait to kill."

Her colleague only nodded. "And you?"

She scowled. "Why do you care?"

"Because I want to understand you. I've never seen you as the bad guy. Sure, you've always been a tad too stern, but as MedAct's CEO, that's necessary. And yet, when I learned the truth about the bond, I couldn't believe you were involved in such a nasty plot."

Fatigue swept over her. "You're talking in riddles again."

Confusion grazed Celise's doll-like features, then she relaxed. "Tell me about him." She nodded toward Nightmare.

Apparently, Jade wouldn't get an answer any time soon. "Do I have a choice?"

"You believe you don't?"

She shrugged. "Well, from my point of view, I'd say I don't, since you kidnapped me and are keeping me here against my will."

Her fellow doctor just watched her, and she didn't like the pity-filled look in her eyes.

Jade cursed to herself. "Fine. I've been fascinated with cyborgs ever since I was young, and it was always my dream to work with them. I watched Nightmare and his Fighters on the news. I grew up with them always being on TV, and I saw their sorrow and fury. They weren't common back then, and they always seemed so torn, especially Nightmare. He was the reason I applied to MedAct when I was old enough."

Celise nodded. "You've always been intrigued by him."

"You could say that." Some part of Jade hated talking about this. She'd never told a soul about her feelings for Nightmare, but for some reason, it also felt good to have it out there. It'd been a long and difficult secret to keep. "I never saw him like the dangerous and deadly cyborg everyone claimed him to be. I looked beyond that and saw a desperate man who needed help. I wanted to help him, and that's still my goal, but I only seem to push him away."

"That's because you don't understand him."

Jade shot her another dark look. "I'm one of the few who understands him. I've told him many times I'd help him find a new bound one, that he can turn to me, but he just boils over and threatens to kill me."

The doctor shook her head. "No, Jade. You *really* don't understand him. You think you do, but you don't. If you knew his story, the *real* story, you'd understand what I'm talking about."

She took a deep breath to calm her growing anger. "I know his story. I've studied it for years in MedAct's files."

"Lies. The files are all lies."

She frowned. "You sound brainwashed."

Celise remained silent for a long moment. "I'm starting

to *believe* you really don't know." Disbelief filled her eyes. "You *really* don't know, do you?"

This was starting to get ridiculous. "Know *what?*"

She shook her head, but it seemed to be more to herself. "No, you can't be that naïve. You're MedAct's CEO. You're in on it. You have to know what the bond really is and what really happened to Nightmare ... unless ..."

"Unless *what?*" she snapped.

"Unless the information was somehow kept from you."

Celise *really was* brainwashed.

A pinch of sadness grabbed Jade. "I can't believe you've ruined your whole life because of a few things the Fighters told you. I feel sorry for you. I really do, but I'm not going to help you out of this mess."

Her eyes narrowed. "You contradict yourself. You say you want to help them, but at the same time, you refuse to hear what they have to say. No wonder Nightmare won't turn to you. He'll never trust you if you think the Fighters are lying."

Jade lowered her gaze. "You're right, but they've never given me a reason to trust them. They only need to see my MedAct badge to turn on me." She scanned Celise. "But not on you, apparently."

Blaze approached with a tablet in his hands. "Nightmare trusts Celise with his life. You have a long way to go if you want to achieve that."

A pinch of jealousy struck her. "How *did* you achieve that?" she asked Celise.

"He showed me the truth, and I believed him."

"And what *is* the truth?" This conversation was starting to grate on her nerves. They weren't getting anywhere, and asking the same question but in a different way wasn't going to help.

Blaze and Celise exchanged a glance.

Jade sighed.

They'd never tell her.

"Whatever. I'm tired and need to rest."

The medic cyborg nodded. "Phoenix will take you back to your room. You'll be supervised the whole time."

She snorted. What did they expect her to do? Run away?

She didn't have the slightest idea where she was, and all the similar hallways were like a labyrinth. Jade was lost without someone showing her the way. She didn't know where the exit was, but she'd managed to figure out one thing.

There were no windows anywhere.

They were underground.

The doors to the infirmary opened and Phoenix entered. He'd been on guard just outside the door.

Jade left the room without another word. She didn't say goodbye. Some of her—justified—rebellious attitude refused to abandon her, and that was good.

She wasn't going to let them break her that easily. Instead, she'd be difficult.

Two could play this game.

"Don't expect much from anyone," Phoenix said as they

51

approached her room.

"Don't take me for a fool." Jade refused to look at him.

"I don't. I'm just saying, not even Celise is on your side."

That was obvious, but her behavior was a huge surprise. The younger doctor was like a completely different person. Where had she hidden all that strength? In the end, it didn't matter.

"Celise has betrayed me and everyone at MedAct," she said.

"No. *You* and MedAct betrayed Celise."

"What the hell does that mean?" The blood pumped in her veins, the rage reigniting.

"Celise discovered MedAct's secret, and she didn't like it." Phoenix remained calm, even if she was about to explode.

"Secret? What secret?"

The cyborg frowned. "Are you really that stupid, or are you just playing with me?"

"I have no idea what any of you are talking about!" she roared as her voice echoed against the walls. The fury had finally exploded.

For a long moment, Phoenix didn't say anything. Suspicion and confusion were written all over his face.

"You owe me," Jade finally said, and poked him in the chest. "I saved your life—twice! If you don't tell me, don't expect a third time."

He snorted and kept walking. "You can't threaten me. Do you really think I want MedAct's hands on me ever again?"

She let out a frustrated breath. "What the heck is wrong with you Fighters? You despise us, as if we were the plague."

"Not far off." He slid around a corner and stopped in front of her door.

A sting filled her heart and made it ache. His words were an insult. Did she really deserve all this? After everything she'd done for them?

"We're only trying to help you."

Phoenix shook his head. "No, you're trying to bind us again, and that's the worst thing you could ever do." He opened the door, beckoning her to enter.

That didn't make sense.

"Why?" she asked as she went inside.

He remained in the hallway with his hand on the door handle. "Because the bond is a poison that's designed to be released into our system the moment our bound one dies."

Her gasp echoed, and she stared as the disbelief in her chest rose to new levels.

"That's one." The cyborg closed the door and locked it, leaving Jade alone with more questions than she had a minute ago.

CHAPTER 7

Jade stared at Nightmare's medical journal. It was filled with numbers, conclusions, and diagnoses, but her eyes were blind to it all.

Her mind was elsewhere.

She raised her gaze to where he lay on the bed in the infirmary.

He'd been taken out from the tank a few hours ago. The chip was working fine, and all they could do was wait.

Jade had been sitting by his bed ever since.

Celise had allowed it, but she was never left alone with him. Her colleague or Blaze was always present, both keeping an eye on her.

Their trust wouldn't come easily, and honestly, Jade wouldn't trust herself if she were in their shoes.

MedAct was the Fighters' enemy, and as the CEO, she was the *main* enemy.

Therefore, it was a wonder she was allowed to be by Nightmare's side, since the surgery was done, and had gone well. She returned to the journal, but still didn't see it.

Had Phoenix spoken the truth? Was the bond really a poison?

Why did the Fighters think that? The copper-headed cyborg had seemed convinced.

She yawned. Spending almost all night thinking about it had done her no good.

How the hell could something like that be true?

It wasn't possible to keep a thing like that from her. Sure, to access the private server at MedAct, she needed the Council's approval, but apart from that, Jade had access to *everything*.

She knew *everything* about MedAct.

They had to be lying, but...what if they weren't? How the hell could she not know about it?

Jade shook her head. She couldn't recall how many times she'd cried and laughed last night from this surreal situation.

Now, her tears and laughter had dried, but the need for answers hadn't gone away.

Far from it.

Instead, determination filled every part of her. If the Council had kept this information a secret, heads would roll.

She had the power to put the Council in their place, and she wasn't afraid to use it.

If the Fighters were convinced of this, maybe there

was something to it. She needed to find the answers, and if possible, help Nightmare. That was, after all, what she'd tried to do from day one, but it hadn't worked.

Because she hadn't listened to him.

Regret filled her.

That'd never been her intention, and yet, Jade had never even given him the chance to see her as a friend.

Instead, they'd been nagging at each other like some old married couple from the start. How the hell could she turn that around?

She sighed and glanced at him.

Two shining angry eyes stared right at her.

She popped to her feet.

He was awake!

"You," Nightmare growled. The pure hate in his expression was unmistakable.

Jade opened her mouth to tell Celise and Blaze, but before even a single word came out, the Fighter's leader flew up from the bed.

His big strong hand wrapped around her throat.

For a split second, she didn't move, only looked into his fierce eyes, trying to grasp what'd just happened. Jade tried to inhale, but no air reached her lungs. She broke out in a cold sweat. Her heart sped into overdrive and she pounded on his arm, desperately trying to fill her lungs.

His grip was like solid rock. Nightmare stood unaffected by her attempts, snarling with pure fury.

He could break her neck if he wanted.

She'd just saved his life, and this was the price?

"I'll kill you," he growled. "I've no idea how you got your hands on me, but I won't allow you to hurt me further."

Running feet came from behind, and Blaze was there. He grabbed the leader's arm. "You're safe! Don't kill her."

Nightmare blinked and peered at the medic Fighter. His rage melted into confusion. He looked around, and recognition filled his gaze. He swayed on his feet. "I'm … home?"

Blaze smiled. "Yes. You've been out for several days. We've been waiting for you to wake up."

He blinked again, and slowly pulled his hand away from Jade's throat.

Jade perched her hands on her knees, inhaling deeply. She started coughing and a burning sensation filled her lungs. She moved away as blood rushed to her face, making her dizzy.

That had been close.

Celise was instantly by her side, worry in her eyes. "Are you all right?"

All she could do was nod.

"For a split-second, I thought I was in MedAct's hands again," Nightmare said with wide eyes.

The medic shook his head. "No, you're home. I promise."

The relief written all over his face was so strong it smacked Jade's chest.

She could only imagine what'd gone through his mind when he'd seen her. She'd seen the pinch of fear in his eyes, as he'd lunged, but his fury had overshadowed it.

Nightmare sat on his bed and exhaled. Then he focused on her. Those shining eyes went icy. "What's *she* doing here?"

"She saved your life," Celise said. "You were shot in the head by a cyborg soldier when we were at the warehouse. Neither I or Blaze could do anything to help you. Your damage was beyond our expertise. Jade was your only hope."

His gaze hardened, but he didn't say anything.

Jade straightened her back. Her lungs were slowly returning to normal. Being able breath felt almost like a Christmas present. "Don't worry," she said. Her voice came out hoarse; her throat had needles in it. "I'm not here voluntarily. They kidnapped me."

He snorted. "Of course. You only saved me because your life depended on it. Don't expect a thank you. You would've left me for dead, if you had the choice."

Jade didn't answer. His words hurt like hell, but maybe that was for the best. Things would only be worse if he discovered her true feelings for him.

Had she really believed she'd be able to gain his trust?

She snorted. What a load of crap.

Celise had made her believe she'd be able to do it, but now, she saw the reality.

Nightmare would never trust her.

His hate for her was just as strong as her love for him.

Jade glanced at her colleague.

The younger doctor stared with wide eyes as if she was saying, "*I can't believe you just said that. Why are you pushing him away?*"

Jade took a step toward the door. "I guess I'm not needed here anymore. Who'll take me back to my room?"

"I'll take you," Celise said.

"You still need to examine Nightmare to make sure everything's fine now that he's awake," Blaze said.

She froze. The thought of touching him now that he was awake was so tempting it was almost impossible to say no, but it wasn't a shocker where Nightmare's thoughts lay when it came to that.

"If she touches me, I'll kill her," he hissed, as if he'd read her mind.

Jade sighed. "You heard him." She moved toward the double doors. "I'm sure he's fine."

"You still need to check," Blaze demanded, obviously ignoring Nightmare's threat.

She slowly met Nightmare's shining eyes.

His pissed off look overshadowed the medic's serious expression.

"Do you expect me to go near him when he's like that? He'll rip my head off."

"No, he won't."

"Whose side are you on?" Nightmare glowered at Blaze, looking angrier by the minute.

A pinch of irritation flashed in Blaze's eyes as he looked at his leader. "Jade's been with us for several days. She's been fighting to save your life. She's been sitting tirelessly by your side ever since she performed brain surgery on you to fix the ruined chip. You're alive thanks to *her*."

Nightmare's jaw dropped. The aggressive aura he usually radiated was back with a vengeance. "You let her sit by my side? You let her *touch* me?"

The medic sighed. "She was never on her own."

"It sounds as if you're defending her."

"I'm telling the truth. Let her do a final checkup. Neither I, nor Celise can understand the numbers and the scans on that level. Only someone who creates cyborgs can."

No one moved.

The air in the room thickened, and Jade expected an explosion any second.

Blaze's words—almost a defense of her—shot surprise all over her body. A feeling of gratitude had followed, but she hadn't allowed it to set.

He wasn't really defending her. He was doing this for his leader, because they all needed Nightmare, and Jade hoped, that deep down, Nightmare understood that as well.

She cleared her throat and approached him with caution.

The Fighters' leader didn't speak, but his pursed mouth and tight fists spoke of what he was really feeling.

If he decided to kill her this time, she'd be dead before Blaze and Celise could stop him.

Only God knew what stopped him last time.

Jade swallowed when she stepped in front of him. Her heart skittered from fear and excitement when she met his strong angry gaze. "You need to take off your shirt."

The rage in his eyes intensified, but he did as asked. He probably wanted to get the exam over with as fast as possible.

She reached for the scanner next to the bed with shaky hands. Trying to not look at him was almost impossible.

Jade had been around cyborgs for years. Seeing their naked fit bodies was a daily routine, and it rarely affected her.

However, seeing Nightmare shirtless got her going in the worst kind of way. Hopefully, he mistook her nervous behavior for fear.

"You're going to drop that thing," he said.

She jerked from the sound of his deep voice. "What?"

His gaze went to the scanner in her hand. "That thing."

She gasped when he grabbed her hand and helped her press the scanner to his naked chest.

A wicked—and way too dark—grin spread on his lips. "You're *my* prisoner now."

Jade's chin dropped, and they stared at each other for what felt like centuries.

Shit.

Shit!

She really *was*!

He was the Fighters' leader after all, and they'd do anything he said.

Celise tensed.

Jade spotted it from the corner of her eye.

The same thought seemed to cross Celise's mind.

"You can't hurt me," she tried. Finding her strength wasn't easy, but she wouldn't let him scare her.

Nightmare frowned. "Why not?"

Jade peered at the scanner still pressed against his chest. His hand covered hers. "Because I'm … I'm …" Stating that she was the CEO of MedAct wouldn't help her one bit.

His dark grin intensified, and he caressed her cheek.

She expecting him to do something, but the touch remained feather-light. It made her tremble, and yearn for more. Weakness filled her knees, but somehow, she remained on her feet.

He leaned closer. "You think you're something?" The Fighters' leader snorted. "You're what I say you are." Excitement flashed in his eyes. "And I say you're *mine*."

CHAPTER 8

Nightmare couldn't believe his luck.

Jade Silva was in his grasp!

The cute, but fierce, doctor was finally where he'd wanted her to be for so many years.

He'd had his eyes on her ever since she took over MedAct after Alexander Fleming's disappearance, the previous CEO, about fifteen years ago.

Deep down, he'd hoped for a better co-operation with MedAct; that Jade would listen to him, hear his story, and understand.

When he'd seen her on TV for the first time, Nightmare had been filled with excitement.

She'd been standing in front of the cameras, wearing her white coat, her thick brown hair in a ponytail, declaring to the world, with her full and kissable lips, that she now was the CEO of MedAct.

Jade had been young; her eyes had radiated with insecurity, but an aura of determination had been there as well.

Then she'd spoken about her plans for the future and where she hoped to take the company, and he'd listened with eagerness, but with each word, he'd died a little bit on the inside.

She'd declared, she had no intentions of stopping the creation of cyborgs. Instead, Jade had decided to take Carolyn Williams' cyborg school to the next level, and make cyborgs more accessible for the masses.

The women who'd applied still needed to have money and stable lives, but they didn't need to be extremely rich anymore.

It was a tough education; the women had to go through psychological tests, background checks, and demands, but also had to learn everything about cyborgs.

Many women failed, but thanks to the changes, more were able to apply. There were more cyborgs out there now than he'd ever seen coming.

After hearing Jade's words, she'd become his instant enemy.

It'd been like that for years now.

She chose to continue Carolyn Williams' work and he'd never forgive her for that.

Carolyn was the cyborgs and MedAct's creator, but the cyborgs never were anything but machines to her.

The world didn't even know about all the awful things

she'd done to him and his brothers. The thought of the bitch made him shiver and clench his fists again. If she'd been alive, he'd kill her.

Jade's beautiful face and strong gaze danced through his head. She gave him a sweet smile, and just like that, the uncomfortable feeling faded away.

Nightmare blinked.

There it was again.

That weird emotion that gently grazed his heart every time he thought of her, or every time they met; that feeling he always chose to ignore.

He shook his head, pushing it away this time, as well.

Celise entered the infirmary with her arms crossed. "I've taken Jade back to her room."

"Where are you keeping her?"

"In room B11."

Perfect.

The room wasn't too close to anything special.

Jade was being kept away from the Fighters who were locked away, but also from the Fighters who weren't.

Celise sighed. "I think we should talk."

He frowned. "About what?"

"We didn't bring Jade here to be your prisoner. We brought her here to save your life."

"Don't worry, dear Celise. I won't hurt her, but I *will* make her talk. The knowledge she possesses can save our lives. I've tried to get my hands on her several times. She's always been just out of my reach, but now, when she's finally here, I will *not* save her from my wrath." Nightmare grinned. "I guess her trust in you became her demise. I'd love to hear how you managed to catch her."

The doctor's eyes narrowed, and for a while, she remained silent, just studying him. "She doesn't know."

He blinked. "What?"

"She doesn't know what the bond really is."

Nightmare stared for a moment, then burst out laughing. "You've got to be kidding me. How can she *not* know? She's MedAct's CEO, for heaven's sake! She knows all their secrets."

Blaze, who'd been sitting by the computer, rose from the chair. "I think it's true. She seems oblivious to the bond's true nature."

His laughter died. "You're lying."

The medic shook his head. "We can't be sure, but much points to it. Think about it. As far as we know, Alexander Fleming didn't know either, and he was the previous CEO of MedAct, but once he learned the truth, he did everything in his power to figure out how to remove the bond." Blaze shifted his weight to his other leg. "What if he and Jade are just puppets?"

Nightmare's fists turned white. "Puppets?"

He nodded. "Yes. Puppets in a bigger scheme, and Jade is, just like Alexander was in the beginning, unaware of her involvement."

"Listen to yourselves. Has she somehow brainwashed both of you?" He snorted.

"I'm totally serious," Blaze went on. "There's more going on here than any of us is aware of. We've been trying to get Jade to tell us about the bond ever since we brought her here, but each time we ask, she just seems more confused and irritated."

Silence filled the infirmary.

Nightmare's gaze shifted from Blaze, then to Celise, only to shift back to the medic again. Words refused to leave his lips, as disbelief filled every part of his body.

This had to be some sick joke, but trying to tell himself that became more and more difficult when their serious expressions remained.

His thoughts went to Jade.

Her cute and sweet appearance could fool anyone into thinking she was an innocent housewife that baked cookies for the neighborhood's kids every day, but the strength in her brown eyes spoke of another story.

The CEO's straight posture and firm lips whispered of what type of woman lived in that fit and small frame of hers.

When Nightmare had seen her for the first time—about fifteen years ago—he'd underestimated her.

He'd thought she'd be easy to play once he'd figured out she continued implanting the bond into newborn cyborgs. Instead, she'd turned out to be a worthy adversary.

He glanced at the door. He needed to find out for himself if what Celise and Blaze said was true.

A pinch of fear filled him.

What if it *was* true?

What if Jade didn't know?

That would turn things around for sure.

Nightmare clenched his teeth and inhaled. Then, he headed for the door.

He and Jade were going to have a long talk, a *very* long talk.

Celise grabbed his arm.

Nightmare halted and met her eyes.

"Don't hurt her. I mean it," the doctor ordered.

He studied her.

She'd gone from a shy and innocent woman to a strong leader in just a matter of a few weeks, since she and her cyborg, Wind had gotten involved with him and his Fighters.

The I-mean-business-look in her eyes made his lips twitch. "I believe you do." He tore himself free from her grip and headed for Jade's room.

CHAPTER 9

Fear filled every part of Jade's body, making her tremble like a leaf. She'd never felt this small. She'd never felt this vulnerable.

The reality of her situation slapped Jade in the face over and over again. Now, she really *felt* the danger that surrounded her.

Now that Nightmare was awake.

Cold chills traveled down her spine and her palms went clammy.

Jade was glad she wasn't standing. Her knees shook way too much.

She stared at the door, waiting for her uncertain future to catch up with her.

It wasn't too difficult to figure out what was coming. She'd seen it in Nightmare's shining eyes. His excitement and anger in the infirmary had been clear.

He was going to make her talk.

No one would interrupt him.

A tear ran down her cheek, but she ignored it. Instead, she curled up on the bed, her gaze never leaving the door.

In a way, it was ironic.

The man she'd loved for so many years would be the one to end her, and for what?

Knowledge she didn't have?

She didn't doubt he'd do it. He'd killed people before. She'd seen it on the news, and it'd always been in cold blood.

Now, he'd do the same to her.

The only time she'd know his touch would be during the torture that was to come. He'd never see her love burn from heartache. He'd only hear her screams, and probably enjoy it.

After all, he'd been ready to kill women and children to make MedAct release the Fighter, Hunter. He'd been ready to kill Shade to remove his bond from his bound one, Phoebe.

Nightmare was dangerous, deadly, untrustworthy, and the dark and strong aura that surrounded him made her really fear him, because now, she was in his grasp.

Despite all that, her heart had started to beat for him all those years ago. Jade had seen beyond his hard shell; had seen the man behind it.

She'd seen his reasoning and his pain. She'd learned to understand him, or at least, she'd thought she had.

According to Celise, she hadn't. That hurt. Not just hurt,

it was as if a big black hole had been carved out in her chest.

A pained whimper left her lips, as she dried a tear with a trembling hand. If she somehow survived the upcoming hours, Jade would do everything in her power to find a way out.

She couldn't stay here.

The door handle went down.

Her heart almost jumped out of her chest. She pressed herself against the wall and watched Nightmare enter.

His eyes were dark, and he wore a smirk. He was ready to have 'fun'.

The door closed silently behind him, but it *felt* like a bomb went off.

It made her twitch and clutch the bedsheets.

Jade's eyes never left him, but the hurt in her heart sang as loudly as never before. The emotions would hurt more than the pain he was about to inflict upon her body.

She couldn't even imagine his reaction if he ever found out how she felt about him.

Worst case scenario, he'd use it against her.

There had to be a way to make him see her in another light, to make him see she wasn't his enemy.

The Fighter's leader watched her for what felt like an eternity before his lips twitched. "They really made things easy for me. All I needed to do to catch you was to get shot in the head. Who could've known?"

Jade didn't say anything. Fear pumped in her veins, but she wouldn't go down easily. She'd fight until her last breath.

"I remember the first time I saw you," Nightmare said and leaned against the chair's backrest, his eyes almost ... serene. "It was on the news, when you informed the world you were the new CEO of MedAct. I liked the innocent but strong smile you shared, but also that pinch of naivety. You had no idea what you were getting yourself into." He crossed his arms. "I had high expectations of you. Me and Alexander Fleming were never close, but we respected each other. So, when he disappeared, and you came into the picture, I'd hoped for something more." He sighed. "But my hope was in vain."

She didn't move. What was this? Why was he talking about the past?

Why wasn't she pressed against the wall with him holding her in a firm grip? Why wasn't he yelling all those questions he had and demanded answers?

Why was he acting calm all of a sudden?

Was he planning to lure her into a feeling of safety before destroying her?

"Do you remember the first time we talked?" he asked.

No words left her mouth. Instead, Jade fixed her eyes on him, watching his attractive but stern face, still waiting for the torture she'd imagined so many times since she'd been taken back to her room.

Yet, she *did* remember their first meeting.

To her, it'd been like meeting a celebrity, because she'd watched him on the news since she was a young girl. How many times had she wondered if there was something wrong with her for pitying him?

Many despised him, avoided him, hated him for what he did … for what he was … but not *her*.

It'd taken the world some time to get used to the cyborgs, but once they were part of society, Nightmare had become a side note in the newspapers.

People started to get used to his antics. They still tried to catch him, but didn't get as shocked anymore when he robbed a store.

He only took food or equipment anyway, and sometimes, people even left things out for him. She did that too once as a child, but when her parents found out, they'd grounded her for a month.

Jade licked her lips. "I remember."

A dark grin spread on his face. "I'm sure I left an impression on you."

"Rather, the gun you pointed at me did."

He shrugged. "I was being careful."

The deep look he gave her stirred something within her.

She should feel uncomfortable, unsure, wary of him, but that fear was slowly subsiding.

He wasn't going to torture her. He wasn't going to hurt her.

At least not now.

"If I'd known how things would turn out, I would've kidnapped you that day," Nightmare said. "I never got the chance to get that close to you again, without the cyborg soldiers around." He took a deep breath. "It is what it is. I wasn't after that back then, but here you are now."

"You broke into my house in the middle of the night. After something like that, moving into an apartment at MedAct was the best decision for me." Her voice was cold as the memories washed over her.

Jade had been tired that day and had taken a shower. It usually calmed her and helped her sleep, but when she'd opened the bathroom door, Nightmare had stood on the other side of the threshold with a gun aimed at her chest.

He chuckled. "The expression on your face when you saw me was priceless. You almost dropped your towel."

She hadn't found it fun at all, but Jade would never forget his amusement when she managed to flash him with one of her breasts from the sheer surprise of seeing him in her room. Heat traveled to her cheeks. "That will never happen again."

His grin faded and his eyes narrowed. Then he sighed again, and shook his head. "We sure are good at hating each other. We could accomplish amazing things if we just worked together, but no. We choose to throw knives at each other instead."

Jade winced. "You want us to work together?"

"That's never going to happen."

The seriousness and lack of emotions in his voice almost stopped her heart. In a way, it felt as if he was breaking up with her, and the pain was difficult to hide, but she pressed her lips together and swallowed the feelings down. She looked away. "Good."

"But you're going to tell me everything. We're going to spend many hours in here talking." His grin returned, and this time, it was frightening. "We have so much to talk about."

"I'll never tell you anything, even if you hurt me." Her hands shook. She pressed them to the bed to hide it, but despite his dark aura, the danger he radiated, she still couldn't suppress his … magnetism.

She was still drawn to him.

It'd taken many years to get to this point, to feel the way she did now. What'd started as pity and a pinch of fear when she was young was now so much more.

Love.

She'd seen his pain, but also his aggression and despair.

Then, it turned into a need of wanting to help him, and before she knew it, she was thinking about him every day.

He began to dominate her thoughts.

Their encounters happened mostly over the phone, and they always managed to piss each other off, but the underlying longing and desire that'd slowly awakened within her, refused to go away.

Every time she'd heard his voice, her heart had flipped.

For years, Jade had denied the feelings, ignored them, but they stayed put. It had taken a lot for her to finally accept them, to accept that she'd fallen in love with a monster.

"Don't worry. I'm not going to hurt you," Nightmare said. "Celise will hate me forever if I do, but I am going to make you talk."

Even if the threat hung in his words, a part of her relaxed.

At least, now she knew for sure there weren't going to be any torture. Thanks to Celise, but did that mean …?

"Would you have hurt me if Celise hadn't forbidden you?"

The Fighters' leader remained silent for a long time.

Deep down, she hoped he'd say no.

That part of her hoped he cared about her, at least a little bit. That part of her also wanted him to see her for what she really was—a woman in love with him.

Instead, Jade was a woman who desperately tried to hide the truth from everyone, especially him.

Celise had figured it out, and Blaze had heard it, but she doubted any of them had told Nightmare.

Nothing in his behavior pointed to it.

"I don't like hurting people," he finally said, "so no."

She flinched. Even if she'd *hoped* for that answer, she hadn't expected it. "I've seen you hurt people in the past. You've even killed."

"Never without reason."

She blinked. "Really?"

He clenched his jaw. "Who do you take me for? I'm not a murderer. I'm a survivor."

His files at MedAct flashed by in her mind, the files Carolyn Williams had left behind. He'd been her first successful creation, and Carolyn had written down every step she'd taken. The files were filled with her failures and successes.

Carolyn had died in a car accident about four decades ago, some even said she was murdered, and Nightmare had disappeared around that time.

No one knew what'd happened to him until he'd suddenly reappeared and started taking in cyborgs who'd lost their bound ones.

They became the Fighters and didn't allow anyone to stand in their way.

There were tons of videos of them robbing places, shooting at police officers, and leaving nothing but destruction behind.

Carolyn's young nephew Alexander Fleming, who'd been just a young boy back then, had taken over MedAct after her death.

The company was run by the Council until he was old enough, but one day, he'd gone missing as well.

His disappearance was never solved, and until this day, no one knew what'd happened to him.

Nightmare flew up from the chair.

Jade winced and pressed herself against the wall.

Was he going to hurt her now?

"Enough of nonsense. It's time for us to get serious."

CHAPTER 10

Nightmare stilled when she flinched. He wasn't used to seeing her like this. He was used to seeing a strong and determined woman, who'd argue with him for days, but her trembling hands and fetal position made him slow down.

Jade really believed he was going to hurt her, even if he'd just told her he wouldn't.

He could use that.

It could make her talk. He could do whatever he wanted to her now.

She was finally in his grasp, his prisoner, and she believed him to be this dangerous, unpredictable, and deadly cyborg that also most of the world thought he was.

In a way, he was, but deep down, he wasn't.

It was just a defense, a defense he badly needed to survive.

Until lately, Nightmare had never had anyone but the Fighters. Now, there was a woman—Celise, a previous

MedAct doctor who'd joined him on his quest. She'd changed things around and made him hope again.

No human had ever trusted him, and yet, Celise did.

She'd even decided to help him, to stand by his side. He would've cried if he'd been able to, but his tears dried a long time ago.

The woman he had in front of him, on the other hand, was a completely different story.

He didn't trust Jade one bit, and Nightmare doubted he ever would.

Fifteen years was enough for him to know the answer to that question.

"I've spoken to Celise." He tried to ignore Jade's fear. "She told me you don't know what the bond really is. I have a hard time believing that, but I'm ready to listen, to hear your side of the story, but I'm warning you. I *will* know if you're lying."

She licked her lips and let out a shaky breath.

His gaze locked on her mouth. He inhaled sharply, clenching his fists.

For some reason, he could barely tear himself away. He'd seen her do that tiny maneuver plenty of times.

She did it whenever she was stressed, but watching her do it now, was like the sweetest aphrodisiac.

His blood pressure rose. His heartbeat increased, and a mad longing awakened in his chest.

"Crap." Nightmare turned away.

That damn bond!

He closed his eyes. Took another deep breath, then a

second one, and a third. Or was it the fiftieth? He breathed in through his nose and breathed out through his mouth.

It helped, but barely.

"Are you all right?"

He slowly turned toward her again with shaky knees.

Some of her fear was replaced with a pinch of obvious worry.

Nightmare frowned. Was she really concerned about him? That was a first. "I'm fine. It's only my bond acting up."

Her lips drained of color. "Maybe you should leave."

He snorted. "Do you think *you* have any say? I'm here to interrogate you."

"And if you lose control? What then?"

"I've been unbound for four decades. I won't lose control just because I'm close to a woman. The bond's acting up because it sees you as a potential bound one. It behaves like this around every woman who isn't a cyborg's bound one. You're not special in any way."

Jade's gaze darkened. "I never said I was."

He winced. Why the heck had he said that?

"Whatever." Without a second thought, Nightmare sat on the bed, facing her, his knee bumping her leg.

She flew off the bed like a burned cat. "Are you crazy!" She gave him an angry glare.

He remained calm, but on the inside, a huge piece of surprise filled him. Why the hell had he sat next to her? "It takes a little bit more to bind me to you. It has to be an intimate touch."

"I know, but I'm not taking any chances."

Nightmare held in a frustrated sigh and pointed at the bed. "Come back here. I'm not going to talk to you when you're on the other side of the room."

She crossed her arms over her chest. "It's a small room. You can hear me loud and clear from here."

He could, but he wanted her near, right next to him. "Do as I say, or I'll make you."

The fear in Jade's eyes was almost gone. It seemed to be replaced with an adrenaline kick and anger. She was ready for a fight.

He shifted on the bed. The bond was starting to get annoying. It wanted him to go to her, to wrap her in his arms, and kiss her to initiate the bonding process.

It made him picture her naked and warm body against his, it made him imagine her reaching for him and inviting him in.

Nightmare inhaled a shaky breath.

Cursed bond. It would never stop tormenting him.

He stilled. There was something else there as well, something that went deeper, something he had a hard time placing.

It was *that* emotion again.

It'd been there for a long time, for years, and for just as long, he'd ignored it, but as he watched her, it started to awaken, and this time, he couldn't ignore it.

The emotion was like a silent whisper within his heart, something that ignited a small part of him.

Her golden skin, thick brown hair, and brown eyes made

it difficult to look away. Jade's cuteness, smallness, but also her fierceness pulled him in like a flower to the sun.

Everything about her lured him in, and strangely enough, nothing of it came from the bond.

The emotions the bond threw at him were raw and primitive, only after one thing.

This emotion, on the other hand, caressed his wounded insides, gently healing him.

It was all *him*.

Nightmare blinked.

What was this?

He shook his head to shake it off, like he always did, and stood. His feet moved of their own accord.

Jade backed against the wall and raised her hand, her eyes wide. "Stop! Don't be a fool."

His lips twitched, but he didn't take another step, and continued watching her instead. Deep down, it was difficult to remain still.

He was so hungry.

He'd been alone for such a long time.

There'd been plenty of times where he'd feared the loneliness would get to his head.

At those times, he spent hours in the corner of his room with his arms wrapped around him, as emotions havocked inside him. He'd desperately searched for some comfort, for some nearness, but only found nothing.

Always that *nothing*.

Because there'd never been anyone out there for him.

The whole world saw him as a monster, a killer, so he

became one.

That he was alone in a room with a physical woman was enough to trigger so many emotions, emotions he'd hidden for so long.

It didn't help that the woman was Jade.

It only made things worse.

He'd held Phoebe, Shade's bound one, in his arms once, to calm the bond. He'd been safe with her, but if he attempted the same thing with Jade, his bond would instantly initiate.

Nightmare pushed his feelings back the best he could, and crossed his arms over his chest, hiding his inner chaos. "If you refuse to sit, we'll just stand here."

Jade didn't move.

"Very well," he said. "Question one. What is the bond?"

She blinked. "What?"

"You heard me." He held onto his seriousness.

"Is this a joke?"

"Does it look like I'm joking? I asked you a question. What is the bond?"

She looked stunned and her jaw slightly dropped. Then, Jade straightened her back. "You know what the bond is." Her voice was dark.

"Do I? According to what I just heard, you and I believe the bond to be two different things. I want to know what *you* know about it."

Her jaw dropped even more. "You can't be serious." She threw her hands up. "Fine then. The bond is a necessary program for you to function, to even live. Without it, there would be no cyborgs. You should know that; since you're the first one."

Nightmare frowned.

She was either being an idiot, or she really didn't know, just like Celise had said.

Her shoulders sank. "Is it true?" Her voice was so low, and a pinch of sadness filled it.

"Is what true?"

"The bond. Is it really a program designed to kill you?"

"So, you *do* know?" His voice went icy, even to his own ears.

"I didn't." Jade shook her head. "Phoenix told me."

He started pacing, frustration awakened. "How can you not know? It's been like this from the start." He glanced at her, only to discover her expression was even sadder than before. "When I heard you were going to take over MedAct after Alexander Fleming, I was excited. You seemed to be a wise woman, but when I learned you continued implanting the bond within every newborn cyborg, you turned me into your enemy. I was so disappointed, because I took for granted that you knew. You *had* to know! You have access to Carolyn's files. She left *everything* behind." He looked at her again, only to see tears in her eyes.

It made him flinch.

Jade dried the tears away.

"Why're you crying?"

"Pressure," she said and avoided his gaze.

Nightmare frowned.

She was lying.

Something else made her cry, but what?

It was hard to say. So many things could be the cause, but in the end, it didn't matter. What mattered was that she was crying, and he *had* to take that pain away.

With a cautious step, he moved toward her.

This time, Jade didn't move away. She didn't try to stop him, but her sob didn't go unnoticed.

"Alexander Fleming gave me access to Carolyn Williams' files a few weeks before he disappeared. She left a lot of information behind about how to create cyborgs, but there was also plenty of information about why the bond was *necessary*," Jade said and met his gaze. "Apart from that, there was nothing unusual, nothing about a poison."

This couldn't be real.

"What exactly did she leave behind?"

"Two portable hard drives, a private server, and a box with handwritten notes."

He clenched his fists. "Are you sure?"

"Of course. I studied everything for days. There really wasn't anything there we didn't already know, but I read it all. I was to become the new CEO, after all."

Nightmare had to turn away, or he'd punch the wall behind her, risking touching her at the same time. "Fuck."

"I guess you didn't like that answer."

"Alexander Fleming never mentioned anything about the poison?"

"No."

"I see."

It didn't make sense.

Alexander *chose* her as the next CEO of MedAct. He must've had faith in her, but maybe Alexander simply hadn't trusted her enough to tell her the truth. He probably hadn't trusted anyone after learning what the bond really was.

Or had Alexander given Jade information, signs, but she hadn't understood them because her mind had been set on a lie?

He stilled.

What if Alexander's disappearance had been planned?

It was starting to seem like it. He wouldn't have given Carolyn's files to Jade and made her his successor just weeks before he disappeared, if it hadn't been, right?

"If what you say is true, then you've been lied to. When I still was in her possession, she had a room filled with information. Everything was well archived, and it was without a doubt more than just two hard drives, a private server, and a box with handwritten notes. The room was filled with computers, notebooks, portable hard drives, and more."

Jade gasped. "I don't believe you."

"Of course, you don't." He went silent for a while. "No matter what I say, and no matter what you say. None of us will believe the other. We're stuck in limbo."

"I have no reason to trust you."

"And I don't have a reason to trust *you*."

Silence filled the room again.

Nightmare sat on the bed.

Blaze's words had started to sound more and more true.

Maybe Jade was nothing more but a pawn in a bigger

scheme. Just like Alexander Fleming.

He recalled Carolyn's working room. It'd been filled with stuff, but it was possible that most of it'd been hidden away or destroyed after her death.

He'd been inside the room plenty of times, either chained to a chair, or chained to the floor—naked.

Carolyn had worked by her desk, ignoring him for hours. She hadn't even spared him a glance, never bothered if he was cold, if he needed something to drink or eat.

As a cyborg, he could withstand more than a human, but even a cyborg would eventually go crazy after several days of that treatment.

It'd been one of her mind-games, and Nightmare had hated and feared every minute of it, because he never knew how they would end.

Most of the time, she allowed him to return to his cell when she was tired of having him there. Other times, she beat him with anything laying around, or used his body for her own pleasure.

He shook his head to get rid of the memories.

Thankfully, Carolyn had no influence over him anymore.

He didn't care about her anymore.

Nightmare was free now from the bond, from the love she'd forced upon him. Not even the feelings that the bond had awakened within him remained.

Once his bond had been sealed away, thanks to the signal he'd created, the signal he'd implanted within every Fighter to protect them from their broken bonds, the feelings had been easy to get rid of.

Now, there was nothing but hate and the desire for a new bound one left.

Too bad Carolyn had gotten such an easy way out by getting killed in an accident. He would've loved to make her suffer, to give her some of her own medicine before ending her awful existence.

Nightmare raised his gaze and studied Jade. She was nothing like Carolyn, but he still didn't trust her, even if it was more and more obvious something fishy was going on behind the scenes.

Something not even *Jade* knew about.

He'd never trust her, but what if he could make her trust him? What if he showed her just enough to prove that he was right?

"You're awfully quiet," Jade said. "Don't you have any more questions?"

"Not right now." He had to think this through.

Worst case scenario, showing her a small part of his life and knowledge could change the Fighters' fates for the worse.

"Good," she said. "Then you can bring me some food. I'm hungry."

CHAPTER 11

The dark look Nightmare flashed made Jade almost flinch, but she stood her ground.

She'd shown enough of fear in front of him.

No more.

He considered her weak already, and would use it against her if—when—he got the chance. That was the last thing she wanted, especially now when she was in his world.

Alone.

In other words, she had to play her cards right.

"You want *me* to get *you* food?" His voice was dark, with a pinch of surprise.

Her heart skittered before it rushed, but she looked him straight in the eyes and raised her chin. "I'm locked up, aren't I? If you won't get it, I'll starve."

Nightmare grinned. "Now *that* would be terrible."

This time, Jade couldn't hold back her flinch. "You'll be

in more trouble than you already are for kidnapping me, if I die."

"Technically, it wasn't me who kidnapped you."

"Technically, yes, but since you're the face of the Fighters, you'll take the blame, so let's start with the food, shall we?"

The leader remained silent; just watched her for a long and painful minute.

Tense excitement filled her as she stared right back. Despite everything, despite him seeing her as the enemy, her attraction for Nightmare washed over her.

He was beautiful, with his dark features, shining eyes, and fit body. Despite Carolyn's bad intentions, she'd created a masterpiece.

He was like a painted canvas Jade couldn't stop admiring.

That was both exciting and terrifying.

Exciting, because he made her heart pound, terrifying because she was far from safe in his presence. Especially when they were on their own. He'd said he wouldn't hurt her, but he had other things in store for her, *for sure*.

Butterflies danced in her stomach, and her body tingled all over as she watched him. The need to touch him, to trace her fingers down his muscular arms was strong, but she reminded herself to stand still, to not approach him.

Every Fighter would blame her if Jade triggered his bond, no doubt assuming she'd done it on purpose. Some of them would likely attack her in pure rage, and Nightmare would attack the Fighters, and the war would be on.

She closed her eyes to shake the feelings off. This wasn't

the right place or time for her emotions to act up.

No, it didn't matter how much she wanted to be in his arms. She could never— literally never—touch him.

Not even if *he* allowed it.

Her chest tightened. She'd been alone for so long.

For years, she'd told herself she didn't date because of work, but deep down, she'd always known.

It had always been because of *him*.

The lump in Jade's throat grew. It was almost impossible to hold back the sob that wanted to break free. Somehow, she succeeded and continued their staring contest.

Nightmare wasn't a fool. He knew what would happen if he touched her, but that pinch of longing in his eyes was unmistakable.

After all, his bond still screamed for a new bound one— like it'd done for about forty years.

The worst part was, his longing wasn't directed at *her*. No, the worst part was his longing was directed at her because she was a woman without a cyborg.

Any woman would do as long as she wasn't a cyborg's bound one, and that stung like hell.

Nightmare finally stood. "Fine," he said, breaking the awkward silence. "Let's go to the kitchen and make you a sandwich."

Jade's jaw dropped. "What? You want me to go with you?"

"Yes." He looked at her, as if his suggestion was nothing special.

She looked around the room. "I thought I was your prisoner."

He nodded. "You are, so running away is pointless. Besides, you'd get lost down here in minutes. Finding a way out would be almost impossible. We're far below ground, and the tunnels go on for miles."

Jade snorted. "Yeah, I figured that much."

"Then, follow me." He opened the door.

She hesitated. "I don't know if this is such a good idea. Every cyborg out there hates me."

His lips twitched. "Don't worry. I'll protect you."

Heat spread in her chest. The thought of him 'protecting her' filled Jade with a pinch of joy, but then reality hit. "You'll only do that because you need answers." The joy faded away.

"I'll protect you because I'm not the monster you believe me to be."

"You're not a monster to me. You never were."

Surprise painted his shining cyborg eyes.

She inhaled sharply. Shouldn't have said that.

Nightmare took two fast steps closer and invaded her personal space.

Jade winced. Instinct told her to move, but she remained where she stood, just inches from him, feeling the heat of his body slowly linger onto hers.

"What exactly am I to you?" he demanded, but there was a pinch of curiosity as well.

She swallowed. "A cyborg that needs help."

"What kind of help would that be?"

"You're lonely, in a lot of pain. A bound one … would help you feel better." Jade had to push the last part of her statement past her lips.

She expected him to explode, like he'd done in the past whenever she'd mentioned a new bound one, but Nightmare stood still.

When his gaze landed on her lips, her heart almost stopped.

He met her gaze again. "And where exactly would you find a woman brave enough to become my bound one?"

Jade blinked. Hadn't expected that question. Was still waiting for an outburst. "Well, I … um …"

He snorted. "You can't even think of one. I'm sure no woman who volunteered to become a Fighter's bound one would ever choose me."

"That's not true!" Jade cringed on the inside. She'd *screamed* the answer.

Suspicion darkened his features. "Tell me her name."

Jade kept her mouth closed.

No woman *had* ever picked him — apart from her.

"If you can't tell me a name, then tell me how many."

Her lower lip trembled. "One."

Nightmare frowned. "That's interesting. It *almost* makes me curious." His expression went cold. "But not curious enough. She's only wasting her time."

His words cut like daggers, but at least, he didn't seem to suspect she was talking about herself. "I think she already knows."

"Good. Shall we?"

Jade's heart pounded.

While he'd been unconscious, she'd been locked in her room to be kept away from the Fighters, or in the infirmary, where Celise or Blaze kept an eye on her.

Now, Nightmare wanted her to follow him to the kitchen, and the kitchen would, most likely, not be empty. "I still don't think this is a good idea."

"Stop being such a coward." He grabbed her and pulled her out of the room.

She gasped and yanked free.

The leader sighed. "Holding your hand isn't enough for the bonding process to initiate."

"Oh." Jade relaxed—a little.

Disappointment shone in his eyes. "You must find the thought of being my bound one repulsive." He grabbed her hand again.

Jade wanted to scream that she wasn't the slightest repulsed, but remained silent. It was for the best if he believed that, but *why* had he sounded so disappointed?

Was there a small spark of interest in him after all?

One he was trying to hide?

No, of course not. It was all in her imagination.

He only reacted like that because his bond demanded a bound one, and she was an unbound woman close enough for him to touch.

She looked at their linked hands as he made her walk down the hallway. If this was harmless, she'd take it. Every second of skin contact with him counted. Who knew how long it would last?

Nightmare led her through long white hallways and after a few turns, she was completely lost, but he walked on with determination.

"Why are you doing this?" she asked.

He gave her a side-look. "Doing what?"

"Taking me to the kitchen. Other Fighters will be there."

"Yes, and you're hungry."

Jade tried to free her arm, but his grip was like solid rock. "They don't like me. You're putting me in danger."

"No, I'm not. I'm their leader, and they'll trust my judgment. We'll go, fix you a sandwich, and once your stomach is happy, we'll continue our little talk."

"And if they don't trust your judgment?"

He gave her another side-look, this time darker.

Jade looked away, unable to avoid the emotional havoc Nightmare awakened inside her every time he looked at her. Even his unpleasant expression triggered a reaction. If only he could *continue* looking at her, but it would be nice if it was in a kinder way. A love-struck gaze wouldn't be so bad.

"I've been the Fighters' leader from the start. No one has ever rebelled against me, because they know they have nowhere else to go, and they know I'm the only one who can help them."

Jade startled at his last words. "How exactly do you help them?"

His lips twitched, but the black in his eyes intensified.

"Give me one good reason I should tell you."

The words hit her hard. The ache in Jade's chest increased, and jealousy swept over her. Why couldn't she gain his trust like Celise had?

It'd been fifteen years, and she wasn't even close to achieving one-tenth of what her colleague had achieved in just a short time.

Sure, constantly arguing with him didn't help, but at the same time, she'd lost count of all the times he'd done things to piss her off.

Like several years ago, when he and the Fighters had robbed a food store. The police had been over-powered easily, and the officer's handcuffs had been used against them.

They'd been cuffed to their cars, and Nightmare had left a note that said, "I hope you like my gift, Jade." He'd even waved with a wide grin toward the store's security camera.

They couldn't continue like this.

"I would like to know." She stayed calm, but shivered on the inside.

With impossible speed, Nightmare released her hand and grabbed her throat, glaring with his shining eyes. There was nothing but darkness and hate in them. "You don't deserve to know."

Jade didn't move. She didn't even flinch when his grip tightened. Instead, she held his gaze, refusing to reveal the fear he'd evoked yet again within her. Her breathing came fast, her body trembled, sweat broke out on her forehead, but thankfully, she could fill her lungs with air this time.

She must've triggered something. What, she didn't know, but why this sudden reaction?

Jade had expected torture and pain when he'd entered "her" room. She'd expected fury and danger, as soon as she opened her mouth, but they'd somehow managed to have a "normal" conversation.

Up until now.

There were two ways she could go from here.

Either react with anger, scream, and make a scene in a desperate attempt to save her life, or ...

Jade raised her trembling hands slowly as she held his gaze.

He could break her neck, and that would be it. He had complete power over her. Nightmare could do whatever he wanted, and she wouldn't be able to stop him. In the end, it'd be her heart that'd hurt the most, but not once did she look away from his furious countenance.

He bared his teeth when she carefully laid her shaking hands on his arm, unable to stop that one tear from running down her cheek.

Pressure, she told herself.

The heat from his bare arm grazed her skin. "I've always been the one fighting for you Fighters." Her statement shook, making it difficult to speak. "*I* was the one who convinced the Council of MedAct to let you live all those years ago." Another tear ran down. "I've been fighting for your survival ever since I became MedAct's CEO. I made them sign a contract promising they'd never try to kill you. It was a contract stating every cyborg's life is precious. Without it, they would've continued hunting you all like animals." She took a shaky breath. "Why do you think we don't do anything to any of you once we catch a Fighter? We never force you, and we only drug you for everyone's safety."

Some of his anger subsided and slid into a frown. "The police still hunt us like animals."

"We've told them not to hurt you, but unfortunately, they don't always listen."

His eyes narrowed. "Why would you do all that?"

"Because you matter to me." Jade swallowed against his grip. That could be interpreted wrong. She needed to correct. "You *all* do," she added. "Don't you see? I've *always* wanted to help you."

Suspicion shone from his shining eyes.

Jade relaxed when he finally let her go. She rubbed her throat but didn't say anything. Her skin was warm and tender from his hold. If she was lucky, she wouldn't have any bruises.

"I don't believe you." Nightmare looked calmer, but the rage was still there.

"I don't expect you to, but it's the truth."

After an angry mumble, he grabbed her hand again and continued down the hallway.

Apparently, the conversation was over.

CHAPTER 12

"This is a very, very, *very* bad idea," Nightmare heard Jade say.

She stared, with wide eyes at the open double doors to the kitchen as they approached. Her steps slowed. The strength she usually radiated wasn't there anymore.

She feared for her life.

It was so obvious, impossible to miss, and it took Nightmare off-guard. He couldn't get used to seeing her like this, so small, so vulnerable … so fragile. It stirred something within him.

A need to protect?

No. Yes?

Could it really be that?

Sounds of male voices from the kitchen filled the hallway. Jade froze and let out a gasp, then pulled her hand, trying to free herself from his grasp.

If he let go, she'd run back the way they'd come, away from the prominent danger lingering in front of them.

They hadn't met anyone on their way to the kitchen, but they were about to come face-to-face with several Fighters, and none of them were fond of Jade.

All Fighters hated Jade.

They hated everything she and MedAct stood for. The company had betrayed them, fooled them, and played with their lives.

The Fighters were convinced MedAct knew exactly what they were doing, tricking innocent women into creating cyborgs that, soon or later, would suffer from losing their bound one.

Cyborgs lived longer than humans, after all.

He stilled.

There was something there. A feeling. It awakened within him, and stirred his bond as it wrapped itself around him like a silky veil, soft, and comfortable.

Yes. He recognized it.

He knew what it was, and strangely enough, one part of him liked it.

The need to protect.

The bond wanted him to protect her.

Jade was doomed without him.

She wasn't in her world anymore. Everything down here was hostile. Every single Fighter. Every single room.

She wouldn't even find her way out without him.

Jade was like a child who needed guidance to understand

the world she'd entered, to learn how to survive within it—and that did funny things to him.

He watched the beautiful brunette tremble. She probably believed this was a punishment; that he'd let the Fighters at her.

She'd been prepared for pain when he'd entered her room.

Nightmare had seen it in her eyes, and he didn't doubt that went through her mind right now.

He used to fantasize about how he'd kill her once she was in his grasp, how he'd make her pay for what she and her company had done to every cyborg who'd been created under her name, but now, when she finally was here, that hatred wasn't there. Instead, there was *something else* …

It pulled him in—no, seduced him, made him drown …

Without a second thought, Nightmare pulled her closer and wrapped his arms around her. The heat from her body instantly hit him in the chest, making him gasp.

Jade tensed and tried to pull herself free. "What are you doing?"

He was unable to answer. He had no idea anyway, but it felt amazing to have her this close. Her nearness made his body shiver, turned his knees weak, and his heart went into overdrive.

He had to be in heaven.

Nothing could feel this good, her warmth, the sounds of her rapid breathing, and her hands on his arms.

It was like a drug he couldn't get enough off.

Nightmare pulled her even closer and leaned down, searching for the place that would spike the heat in his body. It was a promise, something inside him whispered that. It would make him feel so much better. He wouldn't be disappointed.

Her lips.

When he saw them, a fire awakened within Nightmare, a fire he'd never experienced before, and he had no power over it.

It devoured him, fogged his mind as it sang stronger within every cell of his body.

He couldn't resist the pull, the need to kiss her.

As if in trance, he aimed for her lips.

Jade reared back, and her palm jarred his cheek.

Nightmare twitched and straightened his back.

Her dark eyes were slits. "Have you lost your mind?"

He blinked, rubbing his cheek. Had he done something wrong?

How could it have been wrong when it'd felt so good?

Nightmare blinked again, then shook his head. A moment ticked by, then another. It clicked.

Realization washed over him like a splash of ice-cold water. He sobered. A second later, he was two steps away from her.

He'd been so close.

So damn close!

The bond had lured him into a place of comfort, and he'd almost kissed her.

Not once had he considered what the kiss would trigger. All his sanity had evaporated.

Shit.

Maybe he had less control than he'd thought.

"You said holding my hand wouldn't trigger anything, and yet, you almost kissed me," Jade hissed, but held her voice low.

Had she whispered to prevent the Fighters inside the kitchen from hearing?

He clenched his fists. "I won't touch you again." He made his voice cold, but the anger wasn't directed at her.

Nightmare was angry at himself, no, not angry, *furious.*

He'd almost ruined *everything.* It made him nauseous.

He leaned forward and dizziness hit. The need to throw up was overwhelming.

He'd almost jeopardized everything. Literally everything!

Jade placed her hands on her hips. "Look. You don't have to explain anything. I understand what's going on. I assume you haven't been close to an unbound woman for a long time, and that makes the bond go haywire. Am I right?"

Nightmare nodded and straightened his back. "Celise and Faye are safe. The bond doesn't respond to a bound woman, but it does to an unbound one, like you. It doesn't help that a small part of me finds you attractive."

Her jaw dropped. Then she looked away and her cheeks were suspiciously pink. "I guess I should be thankful for that, at least."

"Don't look too deep into it. It doesn't mean anything."

Her expression flashed with something like …
resentment?

"Of course not."

Was that disappointment in her brown eyes?

He'd expected anger, maybe indifference, because why
would she care about what he thought about her?

Instead, Nightmare got a pinch of sadness. It was subtle,
easy to miss, but he still spotted it.

He wanted to ask about it, but it was pointless. That
conversation would only end in an argument he didn't feel
for right now. He was still under the stress his actions had
almost caused. His body refused to calm down, and his bond
screamed inside him.

It wanted him to try again, and to not pull away this
time.

Nightmare stood his ground.

The thought of being bound to a woman again made his
stomach turn.

Carolyn stomped through his head. All those moments
she'd used his body for her own pleasure, all those times
she'd beaten him while he'd been helplessly tied to the bed
or the floor, and all those words … those words of hate and
despise. If she hated cyborgs so much, why had she created
him in the first place?

He clenched his fists. He'd never go through that again.
He'd never be the slave to another woman's "love" again.

Nightmare took a step back, then another, away from
Jade. He'd learned his lesson.

The bond wouldn't get the chance to make him act mindlessly again.

He was on his guard now.

The anger from the almost-kiss still filled his veins. He headed for the kitchen, not caring if she followed or not.

Make her trust him?

Ha!

CHAPTER 13

Was he going to leave her in the hallway?

His steps were fast and angry. "Follow me," Nightmare barked, "and don't try to run. There's nowhere for you to go." He disappeared from view, and the noise of greeting voices hit Jade's ears, making her already stressed heart go into a frenzy.

Follow him?

He had to be nuts!

Unless …

He wasn't stupid. He might be dangerous and unpredictable, but he had all his brain cells in the right places.

This had to be some kind of plan.

There was no other explanation, because he *knew* what it meant for her to be among unbound Fighters.

Apparently, Nightmare had forgotten when it came to

himself—at least for a split-second—but he wouldn't make the same mistake again.

He probably hated her even more now.

It was almost impossible to shake what'd just happened. She'd wanted that kiss so badly.

Jade had ended up slapping him instead. She'd yelled at him, but she hadn't been angry on the inside, she'd only acted like it, because there was no other way. If she hadn't looked pissed, he would've questioned that more.

The image of him leaning over her lips popped back into her mind. Jade couldn't make it stop, and in a way, she didn't want to.

His eyes had been closed, and he'd looked as if he was about to enjoy himself.

That alone had made her tremble, and she was *still* trembling. It'd awakened a deep need, so deep that slapping him had almost been impossible.

Jade had managed to do it in the last second, only to stand on weak legs afterward. It was beyond her how she'd remained on her feet. Her knees shook so much!

The moment still lived inside her, like a side-effect, and it wouldn't go away. If she was unlucky, she'd feel like this the rest of the day.

Laughter came from the kitchen.

Nightmare addressed someone, but Jade had a hard time following the conversation. Instead, the temptation to run became almost overwhelming.

Going in there would be like entering a cave filled with deadly snakes.

The Fighters would stare, their bodies would tense, and even if she wouldn't be able to see it, their bonds would react, and tell them to go to her, to bind themselves to her.

She was an unbound woman after all.

One hundred percent available!

This had to be the worst day of her life. No, it *was* the worst day of her life.

Not even being near Nightmare would change that, because being near him meant danger.

He was like a hostile but tempting environment, and even if he'd done nothing but talk so far didn't mean it'd stay that way. Who knew what wicked plan he'd put together in that deadly mind of his.

"Are you coming?" His voice boomed from the kitchen.

Shit!

Her soul almost left her body at his yell.

She inhaled as much air as her lungs could take, and fixed her gaze on the door. "You can do this," Jade told herself. "I'm not afraid. I'm *not* afraid. I'm the CEO of MedAct, for fuck's sake. Handle this the way you usually do." She clenched her fists and entered the kitchen. She froze right inside in the doorway and looked around.

The room was so big. It was a white well-lit room with plenty of tables and chairs, but the walls were empty, giving it a sterile feeling.

Nightmare stood at the wide counter, preparing sandwiches with ham, cheese, and cucumber.

She locked eyes with four Fighters sitting by a table, eating.

Blaze was there, and Phoenix. Their gazes darkened when they spotted her, but they didn't move. They just stilled.

The other two, on the other hand, jumped to their feet and stared with wild eyes. They were both well-built and attractive Fighters with brown hair. One of them had a more feminine appearance, and the other one reminded her of a bodybuilder. "The bodybuilder" reacted the way she'd expected a cyborg to react.

"What the heck is she doing here?" he growled, and pointed at her.

"I'm interrogating her," Nightmare answered, and seemed untroubled by the tension in the room. "If you can't handle her being here, leave."

The Fighter seemed to walk on needles. His eyes were wide, his mouth low, as he ogled her from the bottom up. The fork in his hand turned into a ball of metal. "Are you kidding me? What kind of interrogation is this?"

"The kind where I make her a sandwich first."

Jade's lips twitched from the leader's smart remark.

He seemed unaffected by the Fighter's reaction, but keeping a calm and neutral air was probably part of his plan. However, he seemed to be expecting *something* to happen.

She, for sure, expected *everything* to happen.

The Fighter looked ready to lunge at her.

"Calm down, Blue," Blaze said, grabbing "the bodybuilder's" arm.

Blue's gaze was fixed on her, and sweat broke out on his forehead. "I don't know if I can. She shouldn't be here."

"Yes, you can. Just take a deep breath and the bond will soon calm."

The huge cyborg licked his lips and jumped from one foot to the other, glaring, as if she was the tastiest thing he'd ever seen.

Jade stood her ground. She hadn't said one single word yet, and she was already creating havoc in the room.

"Why did you bring her here?" Blaze asked Nightmare. "Why did you take her out from her room?"

"She was hungry."

"You could've fed her without bringing her here."

"I could have." The leader still sounded unaffected. "But I wanted her to see."

"See what?" The medic only sounded angrier. His eyes went back to the restless Blue, who seemed ready to bite off his tongue to stop himself from throwing himself at her.

"Us."

Jade looked back at Nightmare. He wanted her to see their world. He wanted to give her insight. Why?

Wasn't she the enemy? Shouldn't he be doing the opposite?

Their home was an impressive place, she had to admit that, but he didn't trust her one bit.

He probably thought she'd run back to MedAct if she got the chance, and report everything she'd been through. That she'd inform the cyborg soldiers, track down the Fighters' headquarter, and attack; take them all down.

Yet, he wanted her to see *them*.

A small part of her rejoiced, but it had to be part of a bigger scheme. She knew him well enough by now.

Phoenix frowned. "Us? I thought you wanted to know what *she* knows, not give her information about us."

Nightmare didn't answer. Instead, he finished the sandwiches and put all the ingredients back into the refrigerator.

Jade remained silent as well. Speaking would only make the situation worse. She stood with her back straight, her jaws clenched, and her eyes constantly scanning the room, preparing for anything.

If Blue gave in to the bond, the only thing that could save her was if one of the Fighters interfered.

Jade could only pray she'd get out of this situation unharmed, and without becoming a Fighter's bound one.

Blue's breathing increased. "Get her out. I'm losing it." He grabbed Blaze's arm, as if to stop himself from going after her.

"If you can control it on the surface, you can control it down here," Nightmare said.

The big cyborg shook his head. "It's different down here. She's so close, so tempting, nowhere for her to run." All his focus was on her.

Crap.

This was going in the wrong direction.

Nothing in Blue's body language indicated he was going to back down. He became more and more tense, his breathing melding into short pants, and his mad glare never faltered.

Nightmare didn't seem to care. He placed the sandwiches on a plate and pulled a bottle of water from the fridge.

Phoenix snorted. "I've no idea what you're planning, but I won't stand here and watch two lives be ruined." He left the room.

Disappointment filled Jade. He could've stayed and helped if Blue snapped, but his actions were clear. He didn't care; none of them did, really.

Not even Blaze was interested. He seemed more eager to save Blue from making a fatal mistake.

It was the Fighter that was important, not *her*.

Of course, he was. She didn't blame Blaze for that, but the knowledge hurt like hell.

How had it ended up like this?

How had she managed to turn the Fighters away when all she'd ever wanted was to help them?

A roar brought her back to the room.

"Calm down!" Blaze yelled.

Ice shot down her spine as she watched Blue, who reminded her more and more of an animal than a cyborg. If she ran, he'd react like a predator and chase her down. Her safest bet was to stand still, do nothing.

The pressure in her body rose. By the end of this day, she'd have, without a doubt, a huge headache. The side-effect from the almost-kiss still lived in her body, and it got company from all the emotions Blue forced upon her.

Fear was becoming her one and only companion.

How many times had she told herself not to be afraid

anymore? That she'd be able to handle anything they threw at her? She'd lost count.

And how many times had she told herself to stand still, to remain on the spot? She'd lost count there as well. The instinct for survival was overpowering.

Her body reacted, before her mind got the chance to catch up, when Blue took a step in her direction.

Jade whirled and fled.

She ran down the white hallways as fast as humanly possible. Frost filled her veins when another roar came.

Seconds later, the sound of someone running after her filled her ears.

Blue, without a doubt.

His heavy breathing gave him away.

Dread washed over her. Cold sweat broke out on her skin. A cry left her mouth.

"No!" Nightmare roared.

She heard the scuffle behind her, but wasn't about to turn around and find out what it was.

Single running steps were quickly joined by other steps.

Jade had never run so fast in her entire life. It couldn't last. Her lungs ached, her heart threatened to give in.

Sooner or later, he'd catch her.

A cyborg was faster than a human, and the never-ending hallways could suddenly come to an end.

She felt Blue's presence build up behind her like a shadow about to swallow its prey.

Then, a hand grabbed her arm.

She screamed, as she was yanked to a halt.

Jade was spun around, and before she got the chance to process what was happening, she found herself in Blue's strong embrace.

The huge cyborg locked her in; made it impossible to get away. He leaned down for a kiss, and she screamed again, until her throat burned.

"You son of a bitch!" Nightmare yelled. "Let her go!"

She met his gaze as he ran toward Blue.

His pure *fury* was beyond anything she'd ever seen before, and the underlying possessiveness filled her with a slight pinch of hope.

He would save her.

He *would*, right?

The leader let out a roar of rage. It echoed against the bare white walls when he went after Blue from behind. He wrapped his muscular arm around the bigger cyborg's throat and pressed, pulling the Fighter back with him.

Blue's body jerked. He released Jade and went for Nightmare's arm. He gasped after air, but his leader twisted his body around with another roar and threw him to the floor.

The "bodybuilder" went down with a heavy thump. He didn't try to get back up, but the glare he gave Nightmare was filled with anger. Then he blinked, gasped, and it all faded away. As if something slapped him in the face.

"Take care of him," Nightmare ordered Blaze as he straightened his back, breathing fast.

Blaze didn't say anything, but his anger toward the leader was unmistakable. The red shine in his cyborg eyes was intense and his lips were pressed together hard. However, he helped Blue stand.

The Fighter groaned and gave Jade a quick look. There was an apology in his eyes. Being thrown around seemed to have helped him snap out of his maddening desire to bind himself to her, but he remained silent as Blaze helped him back to the kitchen.

Jade's body trembled. She let out a sob. Tears gathered in her eyes, but she dried them away. "Are you happy now? Did you achieve what you wanted?"

Nightmare remained silent for a moment, and watched her with unreadable eyes. "I guess I did."

More tears ran down her cheeks. It was too much. She didn't pause to think or slow her pulse. She took two fast steps toward Nightmare and wrapped her arms around him, leaning her head against his chest. The warmth of his body sank in, hard and fast.

She should hate him for what he'd done. She should be furious, and hit him where it would hurt the most.

It was *all* his fault she'd almost become Blue's bound one. He deserved to be in pain, but Jade only pressed her cheek more firmly against his chest.

She needed his nearness and strength instead. It was a twisted and wrong reaction, but she couldn't help it.

He'd saved her in the end, and right now, he was her only haven, even if it meant for only a few minutes.

Nightmare placed his hands on her arms but didn't push her away. "What're you doing?"

"I'm holding you."

A shaky breath left his lips. "Why?"

Jade closed her eyes and shut her mouth. She wanted so badly to tell him what he really meant to her.

Maybe then he'd understand and believe she meant no harm to the Fighters, and that she truly had no idea the bond was a poison, but no, he wouldn't understand.

He'd only use her feelings against her.

Nightmare and the others had to be right about the bond, right?

She still hadn't seen any proof, but much pointed to it. All she had to do was look around to know something was off. "Is your bond reacting to this?" Jade kept her voice low.

"Thankfully, it sees no reason to trigger the bonding process. You're not looking for intimacy, you're looking for comfort, but being near you is difficult. If my thoughts turn the wrong way, so will the bond, but what I don't understand is why you're seeking comfort from *me*." He didn't sound angry, only confused. "I just put you in a dangerous situation, and I did it on purpose."

"I know."

His masculine and warm scent filled her senses. It was a scent she'd gladly inhale all day long. It had a calming effect on her.

"You're not making any sense."

Jade should lie. She should tell him it was because he was

116

her only security down here. No other Fighter would stand up for her, but *he* would because he still needed her.

If she'd told him that, his coldness would return, and the regular angry sparks would start flying between them again, but she couldn't.

She just couldn't stomach those words leaving her mouth. She'd had enough of pain from such conversations in the past.

Keeping him at a distance had been the only way back then.

Now, Jade just wanted him to hold her.

CHAPTER 14

Nightmare had no idea why he'd just lied. Of course, the bond created havoc within him, and *of course,* he felt its need to bond him to Jade; but for some reason, it didn't activate.

Maybe it *was* because she sought comfort, and not intimacy, but at the same time, that wasn't it.

He felt it wasn't, but ...

Something steered his heart.

That *something* pushed the bond aside.

How, he had no idea, but why did it surface now? Why not before when he'd almost kissed her?

With a shaky breath, Nightmare watched the beautiful woman who held him. He only saw the top of her head, but that was enough for that *something*, to intensify.

He'd felt it before over the years and had ignored it, but he couldn't ignore it now. The bond had nothing to do with it. That was weird.

It came from him, and him alone.

Nightmare barely dared to move. A part of him wanted to wrap his arms around her, but what if it triggered the bond after all?

It was way too active for his liking. He should push her away.

They were taking a huge risk, they both knew it, and yet, none of them moved.

Nightmare couldn't for the world understand why *she* did this. She should hate him, she should yell at him, as she usually did.

This was the last thing he'd ever expected.

She didn't even *like* him, then why the hell was she holding him?

Why wasn't she upset over what he'd done?

He'd wanted her to feel the fear she and MedAct had put him and the other Fighters through over the years, to understand what *he'd* been through, but he hadn't expected Blue to snap.

Usually, he was in good control of his bond. That's why it'd come as a surprise when he *did* snap, but Nightmare hadn't in a million years seen the hug coming.

Why on earth did it feel like he'd failed when he had succeeded? Why was he regretting his actions?

She was crying, wasn't she? She'd felt fear. She'd even run. That was the result he'd been after. The idea of making her trust him had quickly gone out the window when his anger had surfaced, and yet, he'd kept to it. For a little while, he'd wanted her to get a small insight.

Then why on earth did it feel like he'd just committed the worst type of crimes?

Nightmare inhaled. He had no answers, but he had to end the hug before the bond initiated. He had to take her back to her room.

He bent down and lifted her up in his arms.

Jade's eyes widened and her jaw dropped, but she didn't protest when he started walking.

Nightmare didn't look at her. He focused his gaze on the hallway in front of them. Looking at her would only make him want to try to kiss her again, and that was the last thing he needed right now.

"Why are you carrying me?" Her voice was low, filled with exhaustion.

"Because you need it."

"Why do you even care?" She pressed her head against his chest.

Nightmare tightened his mouth. "Because you're doing something to me."

Her gaze shot up. "Maybe you should put me down."

"I don't want to." He flinched on the inside.

Why was he doing everything *but* the right thing?

He was supposed to end the hug!

Jade pushed on his chest. "If I'm doing something to you, then you shouldn't hold me. We don't want the bond to trigger."

He gave her a frown. "Then why did *you* hold me?"

She cleared her throat. "Because ... you saved me."

His steps slowed. Had he saved her to save her?

Or had he done it because of selfish reasons?

Seeing her in Blue's arms had triggered a jealousy he'd never felt before. "As I said earlier, don't look too much into it." Nightmare made it a cool snap.

She snorted. "Back to hating me, are we?"

He didn't answer. Instead, he turned around a corner.

She felt good in his arms. He could carry her like this for hours and never grow tired. He didn't mind having her this close; not at all.

Instead, he welcomed it ... and that was a dangerous thing to do.

Strange.

Just hours ago, everything had been so different. Jade had always been strong and powerful in his eyes. She'd always been a worthy foe, but now, when he'd seen her fragile side, he wanted nothing more but shield her from everything.

There it was again. The need to protect.

Stupid bond.

Jade remained silent for a long moment. "Is it true?" Her voice was low.

"What?"

"That the bond is a poison?"

He met her gaze.

Why was she asking this again?

Did she need another confirmation?

There was a huge mix of emotions in her eyes. Everything from sadness, to shame, and disbelief. Telling her she'd already asked would do her no good.

"Yes."

She let out a sob. "I can't believe it. How could I have *missed* a thing like that?"

Suspicion awakened within him. "I'm not completely convinced you're telling the truth. It's beyond me, how you or any of the MedAct doctors aren't aware of this. After all these years, I was sure you knew."

"I swear to you. I never knew."

There was sincerity in her eyes, but his distrust didn't ease. For all he knew, she was acting.

"Don't worry, sweetheart. I'll give you a chance to prove it, and if you're telling the truth, I'll show you what I, and every Fighter with me, have known for years." Nightmare stopped in front of the door to Jade's room. Without putting her down, he opened the door by pressing his thumb against a metallic plate next to it. It wasn't difficult. She wasn't heavy, but a heavy feeling filled his heart as he entered the room.

He had to let her go now.

"You can put me down," she said when he didn't move.

He didn't say anything. Everything inside him grew to a massive protest. His arms would feel so empty if he put her down.

She snapped with her fingers in front of his face. "Hey! Are you still there?"

Nightmare blinked and met her gaze. "What?"

"You drifted away there for a moment, just staring at the wall."

He cleared his throat. "I'm good."

"Then why aren't you putting me down?"

He opened his mouth, but no words came. No answer would be good enough, because he couldn't even explain it to himself.

All he knew; having her in his arms was the sweetest healing for his scarred soul. "Are you angry I'm not letting you go?"

Her lips twitched. "Not really." Jade leaned her head against his shoulder and closed her eyes. "I don't want to act anymore."

Nightmare frowned.

What the heck did that mean?

His gaze trailed to her lips. He froze and held his breath, but was unable to stop himself from drowning. He stared, his gaze fixed, couldn't pull himself away.

There was no bigger temptation.

A loud gasp left his mouth.

The bond.

It went off like an explosion.

A wild and intense desire for the woman in his arms erupted within him.

Dizziness hit and he wobbled on his feet.

The bond wanted him to try to kiss her again, to bond himself to her.

His body started to shake and moisture dotted his forehead. With a speed he didn't know he had in him, Nightmare put her down and backed away, panting. He still couldn't tear his eyes off her. "Fuck."

"What is it?" she asked, worry in her expression.

He didn't answer, couldn't.

Instead, he fled the room.

CHAPTER 15

Nightmare had to walk away, and fast!

If he stayed another minute, he'd do something he'd regret for the rest of his life. This was the second time his bond had reacted like this, in the matter of an hour, and it was *all* his fault.

He just couldn't stay away from her.

Nightmare clenched his fists, anger boiling up, filling him from the inside out.

What the heck was wrong with him?

What the heck happened to him whenever he looked at her? Why did she pull him to her like this?

It was strange because this wasn't the bond's making, that much he knew, but *this feeling* activated it.

The first time he'd noticed it was about fifteen years ago, on the news when Jade had presented herself as MedAct's new CEO.

His heart had fluttered, and the feeling returned every time he saw her.

When she continued implanting the bond into every newborn cyborg, the fluffy feeling had turned into anger and disappointment.

He'd started to hate her instead, and their chaotic relationship had been the only fact, but deep down, those butterflies in his heart had never really gone away.

Now, when she was in his hands, under his roof ... under his protection ... they fluttered more than ever before.

"Fuck!" He hurried down the hallway before he punched a hole in the wall.

Nightmare had had enough for the day, and he'd barely started interrogating her. His so-called "interrogation" had turned into something else, but at least now, he had a hunch of what was going on.

Blaze's words came back to him. Much really did point to Jade not being aware of the bond's true nature, but that still didn't sit right with him.

As MedAct's CEO, she *should* know.

Maybe she was being played. Maybe Alexander Fleming had been played, too. As MedAct's previous CEO, he should've known as well, and yet, just a few months before his disappearance, he'd started to act unusual and stressed.

Nightmare and Alexander were never friends, but for some reason, the man had given him the complete codes to the female cyborg program. He'd even given him an algorithm that was supposed to remove the bond for good.

He'd used it to create a signal— a signal he'd later used on the newborn cyborg Shade to remove his bond from his bound one Phoebe. To his surprise, it hadn't worked. It'd almost killed Shade, and no matter what anyone thought, that had never been Nightmare's intention.

All their hopes lay in the female cyborg program now. The missing piece had to be there.

Nothing would stop him.

He'd start with proving to himself Jade didn't know what the bond really was. *If* she didn't know, and *if* she was being played, then maybe, just maybe, he'd be able to turn her into a valuable asset, like he'd done with Celise.

With determination, Nightmare flung up the doors to the infirmary.

Wind, Celise, and Blaze were gathered there. They looked up abruptly, as if he'd interrupted a secret conversation.

The medic rose from his chair, anger boiling in his red shining gaze. "What the hell do you think you're doing?"

He approached but remained unaffected by the Fighter's sudden outburst. "I said I would make her talk, didn't I?" He crossed his arms over his wide chest.

"By freaking her out?"

"MedAct uses love to control cyborgs. I use fear to control humans."

Blaze snorted. "And has she told you anything?"

"Not yet, but I'm starting to believe what you all told me. To be absolutely sure, I'm going to test her."

Celise stood. "Blaze told us what happened. Is Jade all right?"

"She's fine, just a little bit shaken. Stop worrying so much about her. She's not your concern."

Her eyes narrowed. "What were you thinking? Taking her into a room filled with unbound Fighters is like asking for trouble."

"I knew what I was doing," Nightmare snapped.

"It didn't look like that to me, when Blue went after her," Blaze growled.

He clenched his fists. "He's usually in good control."

Blaze threw out with his arms, his frustration intensifying. "Well, he wasn't this time!"

"Stop questioning my motives!" Nightmare roared, fury burning in his veins. "She will suffer, if I say so! She will do what I tell her to, or she'll face the consequences! Jade belongs to me, and no one will touch her without my permission. She is mine to touch. *She is mine!*"

Silence filled the infirmary.

Six pair of eyes stared, as if he'd just grown another head.

He stilled, peering back. His words dawned on him.

Worry filled Celise's eyes. "Did something happen between you and Jade, Nightmare? You're acting unusually possessive."

He inhaled. The last thing he wanted to admit was he'd almost become bound to Jade—twice.

They'd forbid him to visit her again, even if he was the Fighters' leader, and even if he was the one who made the final decisions.

"Stop imagining things," he told Celise. "She's nothing

more but a tool. I finally have her where I've always wanted her to be, and you've no idea how good that feels. I'm going to squeeze everything out of her."

The doctor's lips turned white. "You promised you wouldn't hurt her. She saved your life."

"And that's the only reason she's still breathing. That, and because I need answers."

She paled. "You'd kill her?"

"Yeah, he would," Wind said. His expression was cold. "I remember him saying that in the abandoned house when he kidnapped Shade."

Celise paled even more, tears building behind her eyes.

Nightmare sighed. "That was then. Now, I see a potential ally in her, *if* she's telling the truth."

The tightness in her face eased, and a calm feeling settled in his chest. He had to admit, he was fond of the little doctor. She was cute.

He was also forever grateful to her. She'd done so much for him and the Fighters already, even if it'd been just a few weeks since she'd come into the picture. He couldn't allow her to turn her back on him. He needed her, more than she imagined.

"I'm going to test her," he told them. "I've studied the bond's code for years. I got my hands on it a long time ago, before escaping MedAct. I might not know how to use it or how it works, but I'm going to show it to Jade and make her tell me where the poison is located."

"And what if she just pretends not to find it?"

Nightmare straightened his back. "I'll be pointing a gun at her head and threatening to push the trigger if she dares to lie." He raised his arms when Celise gasped. "Relax. I won't hurt her. I already promised you that. Besides, she's more precious alive than dead."

The doctor sat with a deep groan. "You're too much for me to handle."

His lips twitched. "Don't worry, sweetheart. Wind will fill up your energy levels before you fall asleep tonight."

Celise jerked and gaped. A peachy color broke out on her cheeks before she turned away.

"Enough." Wind stood. "You better stick to what you promised, or I'll take Celise away from here, and you'll never see her again."

Nightmare could open his mouth and threaten Wind back, forbid him to take his bound one away, show the cyborg hell if he tried, but he didn't move.

Threatening Wind meant losing Celise for sure, and that was a future he didn't want to find himself in.

He stretched out his hand toward the cyborg. "You have my word."

Wind studied him. Without a doubt, judging him. The disbelief was obvious, and it remained even when he took Nightmare's hand. "You better."

He nodded and glanced at Blaze. "I left the sandwiches I made for Jade in the kitchen. She's hungry. Bring them to her along with a bottle of water."

The medic winced. "Why me? Why don't you do it yourself?"

"Because I'm tired, and I'm going to sleep. Just do it." Nightmare left the infirmary before Blaze had the chance to answer. He went to his room.

He really was tired, but telling Blaze the real reason wasn't on his list. He needed a good night's sleep to shake the feelings Jade's presence had awakened within him. A few hours of deep sleep would do him good, and prepare him for what was to come.

He'd be able to be near Jade again without problems.

He'd be strong, determined, prepared. It'd be a piece of cake.

Nightmare hoped.

CHAPTER 16

Jade paced the small room, her gaze barely leaving the floor. She hadn't slept much, and it was hard to keep her eyes open. The fatigue made her groggy, and what the day had to offer, was still to come.

Celise had paid her a visit early in the morning. She'd brought breakfast, and later, Jade had been allowed to take a shower further down the hall.

Now, all she could do was wait for Nightmare. After the number he'd pulled yesterday, who knew what awaited her.

She shivered.

Yesterday had been a disaster. Would today be better?

Or would it be another disaster?

Yesterday hadn't been that bad at first. She'd expected a lot worse, until he'd taken her to the kitchen. If he hadn't stopped Blue, she would've been his bound one by now.

More tremors went down her spine, and into her limbs.

The thought made her nauseous.

She would've never forgiven Nightmare if it would've ended that way.

Jade stilled.

Why had he saved her?

Had she really seen a pinch of possessiveness in his shining eyes? Or had that been her imagination?

She clenched her fists.

Why was all this so confusing? She was intimately familiar with how cyborgs functioned. She understood their programming and reactions, so logically, his possessive behavior was no brainer.

He was a cyborg, she was an unbound woman.

That equaled the bond going amok. Easy. Problem solved. Period. Dot, and so on.

And yet ...

Deep down, she *hoped* it meant something else. Deep down, she hoped he'd saved her because some part of him cared about her.

At the same time, he'd *caused* the situation.

Jade let out a frustrated puff. "Crap," she said. "I'm looking way too much into this. I'm only causing myself unnecessary pain."

The door flung open, making her wince.

Nightmare entered the room. He gave her a dark glare as he closed the door behind him.

She inhaled.

His shining eyes sparked with anger and frustration, but

also with determination. He was a man on a mission, and he'd do anything to reach his goal. "Sit," he said with a strict voice and pointed on the bed.

Jade obeyed, almost a little too fast, her gaze never leaving him.

His lips twitched, but the dark expression took over again fast. Nightmare grabbed the only chair in the room and set it in front of her before sitting. He had a laptop in his hands. "We're going to play a little game today. No more joking around. I have tons of questions." He pulled out a gun from his back pocket and pointed it straight at her head, "and you're going to answer all of them. Am I making myself clear?"

Her heart almost jumped out of her chest. So much for thinking there'd been something else in his possessiveness.

No, now she knew.

She'd imagined it all.

Damn, it hurt.

Jade held back a tear. "Ask. I won't lie."

"I'll be the judge of that." He handed her the laptop. "Open it."

She didn't dare to do anything but obey. It was powered up, and showed a sequence of numbers and letters on a black background.

"What do you see?"

She studied the screen for a moment, then shot him a frown. "How come you have this? This is the code to the bond's program." Jade scrolled through it. "You have the whole code. How's that possible?"

"Take a closer look, and tell me when you find what's wrong with it." He avoided her question.

She blinked. "I don't need to take a look. I know the code inside out."

His lips thinned. "Do it anyway," Nightmare hissed.

She didn't object again. She didn't dare.

The leader of the Fighters meant business, and she didn't want to make things worse than they already were.

She could only hope he wouldn't gunshot her, but who knew. He'd threatened to kill her many times before.

Jade focused on the screen, scrolling through the code. She had no idea what she was looking for, but she wasn't stupid.

He wanted her to find what was wrong with the bond, what triggered the poison to be released into a cyborg's body when his bound one died.

After all the things she'd been through these last few days, and everything else Nightmare had put her through, she didn't doubt anymore. Jade still hadn't seen any evidence, but she doubted the Fighters would go on like this, year after year.

There *was* something wrong with the bond.

Her heart refused to calm as she searched the code a second time, and then a third, and fourth. It was like trying to locate a needle in a haystack, but the code was exactly as she'd learned it should be.

Nothing was different, nothing was wrong, and

Nightmare wouldn't like that.

She swallowed, and met his gaze with worry running through every cell in her body.

"You don't see it, do you?" he asked with a surprisingly calm voice.

"It looks just as it should." Her voice trembled.

He sighed. "I see. They taught you to not see where the poison is, did they?"

"Look." Her voice shuddered even more. "I know how the code works, how it functions, how it's put together. If a poison is hiding in there somewhere, then it's so well hidden, dozens of MedAct doctors aren't able to see it."

Nightmare nodded. "Some part of me wants to believe that you really are unaware of the bond's true purpose."

"I am, I swear."

"There's only one way to find out."

Jade blinked. "What do you mean?"

He stood, pushed back the safety on the gun, and pointed it at her again. "I will count to five, and if you haven't found the poison by then, you'll die."

Her gaze shot to his, and it felt like he'd just punched her in the stomach. "Are you serious?"

"I guess you'll soon find out." He moved the gun closer. "One."

The disbelief intensified, and she kept staring at him instead. Tears ran down her cheeks, sweat broke out on her skin, and her body started to shake.

Her love for him shattered into tiny pieces, thousands of

needles tore her apart as her heart broke.

She'd never known this kind of pain existed. Her head spun, her gaze went fuzzy, and her body warmed, as if a fever had suddenly come over her.

A small part of her had hoped he'd been lying about shooting her, a small part had hoped he cared, but now she knew better.

"You're wasting time," Nightmare said. "You should be looking at the screen, not me."

"Please … don't". Her lower lip wobbled, her chin shivered even more.

"Two."

"Damn it, Nightmare! I don't know what to look for!"

"I don't believe you. You're in on it. You said it yourself, you know the code inside out. That means you know how to locate the poison, so locate it. Now."

He never raised his voice, but the pure and terrifying fear he sent through her was enough to make her break out into hysterical sobs.

Her strength was washed away.

He'd managed to break her down completely.

"I'm not lying!" The terror made it impossible to remain calm. Any calm she'd had abandoned her for good.

"Three."

"Shit." Her hands jarred, as she frantically started scrolled through the code once more, but her hands shook so much it was impossible to hold them still. Her whole body was working against her. She went in blind, just scrolling, searching desperately after a way out.

There was nothing there.

Just the code she'd always known, down to the letter, and yet, she searched. For what, Jade had no idea, but she searched, how desperately she searched!

Anything to get away from the gun and his hate.

She dried away a tear, but replacements kept running down her cheeks.

Nightmare didn't seem to care about how he affected her.

His expression remained cold and focused on what he was doing. Not even a muscle twitched in his face to indicate he might feel bad.

There was only pure determination.

He really did hate her.

There'd never been any love for her in his heart. Every time she'd thought she'd seen something indicating he cared about her had been a lie.

It'd all been in her head.

"I swear to God. There's nothing here!" she yelled.

"You're not trying hard enough."

"I've looked it through like seven times. I'm telling you, there is nothing there!" Her desperation rose to new levels.

"I don't believe you!" he roared, pressing the gun against her forehead. "Four!"

Jade let out a desperate cry. She scrolled again, but the distress blinded her even further, made it impossible to see the code.

All she had was unimaginable terror inhabiting every part of her body.

The whole world spun, the tears didn't stop, her eyes were hot and sensitive; her heartache intensified.

She'd die from the shock and pain before he'd even get the chance to fire the gun.

"You'll be dead soon, Jade," Nightmare threatened. "You'd better find it."

"There's nothing here! How many times do I have to tell you that?"

Fury masked his handsome features, melding his face into a predator with only one goal on his mind—to kill. "Five!"

Boom!

Jade screamed. She threw the laptop away and curled up, expecting agony to tear her into pieces.

It had already shredded her emotionally, but now it would be physical as well, but as the seconds ticked by, and no pain came, she stretched out her limbs and looked herself over.

There was no blood, no hole in her anywhere.

She looked at the wall behind her. A big hole, that hadn't been there before, decorated it now.

He'd fired the gun, but not *at* her.

Jade glanced at Nightmare with still-tear-filled eyes.

He wore a smirk. "You've convinced me. You have no clue about the poison." He put the safety back on the gun and tucked it into his waistband at his back.

"What?" Her chin still tremored, her body shook, still tense, still expecting the worst to come.

"If you'd known, you would've told me so before I'd counted to five to save your life, but you didn't. Not even once did you indicate you knew. You were consumed by fear. Not even a professional actor would've been able to do so in this kind of situation, and since you're no actor … I believe you. You're a pawn, a completely clueless pawn who's involved in a game she has no idea of."

"What?" she said again. Nothing else came out.

Nightmare grinned. "Don't worry. I wouldn't have actually shot you. I was just testing you."

Jade blinked and wiped away her tears. They'd stopped, but her eyes were sore and would probably be so for hours. She'd never cried like this before. To make it worse, she had slight headache.

Her head still spun, but as everything slowly started to sink in, she couldn't stop the anger from coming over her.

It'd been too much.

He'd crossed a line, and he'd pay for it.

Jade flew up from the bed and swung, slapping him hard on the cheek.

Nightmare's head flung to the side and he groaned.

"You son of a bitch!" she yelled all she had, so much her throat started to burn, but she didn't care. "I hate you! Do you hear me? I hate you! I've been patient with you all these years, but no more. You'll pay for this!" She didn't give him a chance to recover from the hit before she delivered another, and another … and another.

Nightmare raised his hands to protect himself, but that didn't stop Jade from kicking and biting him.

She went at him as a crazy cat, clawing, biting, kicking, and pushing him as every last piece of the fear he'd awakened left her.

"Damn it, woman! You've completely lost your mind." He tried to grab her hands, but she twisted her body and went at him again.

"It's all your fault! *It's all your fault!*" She clawed his arms, that were already filled with scratch marks. She didn't care if she caused him any pain. He deserved every bit of it.

"What on earth are you talking about?" Nightmare jumped to the side. "Stop kicking me!"

Jade didn't obey and delivered her fifth or sixth kick.

For some reason, he didn't hit her back. He only defended himself.

"It's all your fault I fell for you! It's all your fault that I'm in love with you. Damn it, all I ever wanted was you to hold me. I wanted to be the one you'd turn to, the one you'd find comfort with. *I* wanted to be the one who you'd thought understood you, but no, you just never saw that. *All I ever wanted was you to hold me! Do you get that!*"

His shining eyes went huge. "What did you just say?" Shock was written all over his face.

Fury pumped in Jade's veins. "Are you deaf? I told you I love you, but you've just destroyed that love. A small part of me always searched for that small part in you to show me you cared about me, but I got my proof today. You're a monster, and I will hate you forever."

Nightmare blinked and paled. "Are you messing with me?"

"Does it look like I'm messing with you?" She wanted to fix her hair, but her arms were too tired from all the chaos. She didn't need a mirror to know she looked a complete mess, and the few strands stuck to her face irritated her. It intensified her fury.

He stood paralyzed for a long and silent moment before he took a chest-heaving breath. "My mind wants to say I don't believe you, that you can't possibly be in love with me, but your words and actions tell me otherwise."

"You know, I don't give a shit what you think. I stopped caring the moment you pointed the gun at me."

"I've pointed a gun at you before."

"That was under other circumstances. This time, I'm your prisoner, with no cyborg soldiers defending me."

Nightmare inhaled again. "How long?"

"From the start." There was no point holding back anymore. Jade might as well tell him everything now that she'd started. It had slipped out, but it didn't bother her anymore that he knew. "I never intended to tell you. I planned to take it to the grave, but I guess destiny had other plans."

"Fifteen years," he said in a low voice. "You've loved me for fifteen years. I never knew. I never saw."

"I never showed."

Silence filled the room.

Their eyes met and held.

Nightmare's gaze lowered to her lips, and for a split-second, she saw it again, that emotion she knew now was only her imagination.

That indication of longing and desire, that indication of needing *her*, and not needing her because she was an unbound woman.

It was him just being confused, and nothing more.

A sudden bright light filled Jade's vision, making her wince.

She rubbed her eyes.

What'd just happened?

Did the light on the ceiling explode?

She looked up, but it was difficult to see. Her eyes were blinded by all the stars in front of her eyes. Eventually, she managed to blink them away, and when she looked again, the sealing lamp seemed fine.

Where had the flash come from?

Jade looked back to Nightmare, who stood frozen. His gaze was set on her, but he wasn't looking *at* her. Instead, he seemed far away.

Alarm, mixed with curiosity, washed over her.

What was he doing? Had something broken? Hadn't he recovered fully yet after all?

Jade peered closer.

His cyborg eyes shone so brightly!

A cold chill traveled through her. "Oh, my God."

His eyes had flashed …

… and he hadn't even touched her.

CHAPTER 17

Jade pressed herself against the wall. A tightness grew in her body, and shivers continued traveling down her spine, but all she could do was stare at Nightmare, and wait for all the hell that was about to break loose.

He remained still for a long moment. His eyelids started to flicker, and his eyes searched for something to focus on. He panted, loud gasps left his mouth, and his chest heaved.

Pure confusion shone on his whole face.

She cringed on the inside, wanted to crawl into a ball, but Jade remained still. The last thing she wanted was to trigger a reaction explosive enough without her making it worse. Jade screamed on the inside, hoping desperately someone would hear her silent cry.

Maybe someone had heard the gun go off and would come running.

More tears were born and spilled.

How the hell could this have happened?

He hadn't touched her for heaven's sake!

Telling him she loved him couldn't possibly have triggered the bonding process.

Yet, here Nightmare stood, as if paralyzed, distant in his gaze, as if still unaware of what'd happened.

That was just as unbelievable.

His eyes had flashed.

Initiating the bonding process.

With her.

With *her*!

Oh, my God!

If he'd hated her before, it was nothing compared to what was coming her way now.

Nightmare frowned and tilted his head slightly, as his gaze finally locked with hers.

The confusion was still there.

He tried to say something, but no words came out.

His frown deepened instead.

His long-lasting confusion was not good. Nightmare seemed unable to make sense of what'd just happened, probably because he'd been unbound for so long, and it'd happened so suddenly, taking them both by surprise.

Any minute now ... it would click.

And it did.

His whole body went taut when realization flashed by in his shining eyes. He gasped, and horror filled his expression.

He staggered back, as if *she'd* shot him, with his hands

pressed against his chest. A sobbing sound left his mouth, a sound of despair, pure terror, confusion, and chaos. He fell to his knees. Nightmare's huge hands shuddered as he wrapped them around his head and shook it violently.

Another sound left his mouth.

This time it was a roar, filled with rage and all the emotions he'd held back for forty long years.

The door flung open.

Blaze stopped in the doorway with wide eyes.

Celise was just behind him.

"What the hell is going on?" He looked around, met Jade's gaze, then looked at his leader. "Nightmare?"

Jade reacted before her mind understood what she was doing. She pushed the cyborg medic and her colleague out from the room. "Get out, now!"

They ended up in the hallway where a small crowd had started to gather.

Wind, Silver, and Faye were there as well.

All the Fighters approached slowly, some looked with worry at the door to her room, while others watched her.

Nightmare didn't seem aware that she'd left the room.

That came as a huge surprise.

As a newly bound cyborg, his instinct should be to be by her side, no matter what. He should want to seal the bond, but when her gaze turned to him again, he was still on his knees, holding his head in his hands, vibrating hard.

He was fighting the bonding process.

He refused to accept it.

Jade's heart broke again.

It was so hard to watch him like this.

Celise approached. "What happened?"

She gave her a tear-filled look. "His eyes … flashed."

It was as if all air was sucked out of the hallway and got replaced with pure hatred. It radiated at her from all directions, from every Fighter. It was mixed with pure shock and confusion, but the hatred was strongest.

So strong it made her knees weak.

Silver grabbed her shirt, and pressed her against the wall. "What did you do?"

His roar echoed in Jade's ears, but she didn't fight him. "Nothing. He didn't even touch me." She kept her voice calm, but she was unable to stop it from trembling. "I don't know what happened."

"Liar!" He pressed her harder into the wall.

Jade groaned. She'd have bruises later.

Celise pushed Silver away. "Let her go. Hurting her won't help." She turned to Jade. "Are you sure that's what happened?" Her eyes were serious.

Jade nodded. "I'm sure."

Nightmare let out another desperate-filled roar and everyone turned their focus to him. He rose to his feet, grabbed the wooden chair, and smashed it against the wall with another loud roar.

She jerked from the sound.

He went crazy on the rest of the innocent furniture in the room.

No one stopped him, as he tore the linens to shreds, and ripped the pillow to pieces, or when he ripped the mattress in two, and stomped his foot through the bed's wooden frame.

Pure madness lingered in his eyes, and the shine in them intensified by the minute.

"Oh, my God." Faye put a hand over her mouth. Her gaze was filled with disbelief. "His eyes are shining the way yours did after the first flash," she told Silver.

Her cyborg nodded with a grim expression. "So, it's true. His eyes flashed."

From the corner of her eye, Jade didn't miss the dark glare Silver sent her way, but she couldn't tear her eyes from Nightmare.

She should be there for him. Try to help him.

Her feet moved in his direction.

Jade came to a halt when someone grabbed her arm. She spared Celise a look over her shoulder.

"Don't go in there. He'll tear you to pieces."

"He needs me."

The doctor nodded. "He does, but not right now. He's fighting the bond, and it will take some time for him to accept it."

She clenched her fists. "I know." Her voice was low. Helplessness washed over her.

This was all her fault.

He'd never forgive her.

Nightmare threw away a wooden leg, and stormed out

from the room, pushing his way through every Fighter who stood in his way. He took off down the hallway.

"Shit," Blaze said. "I'll take care of this. Don't follow." He ran after his leader.

Jade had expected this to be a difficult day, but she'd never expected this. How blind she'd been.

Things were worse than ever, but why had his eyes flashed? Was it even possible for a Fighter's eyes to flash from just standing near an unbound woman?

Not according to what she'd learned.

Jade dried her eyes for the fiftieth time, with a shaky hand. Her knees were weak, and her body was heavy from all the stress, but there was also a small pinch of joy. It was *so* not suitable for the situation, but she couldn't help it.

To become Nightmare's bound one had been an unspoken dream for a long time. She'd denied it every time it'd crossed her mind. She'd barely dared to think it, but now, it had come true.

Just not in the way she'd imagined.

Jade had hoped he'd come to her of his free will, but that would never happen now.

She swallowed and looked around, locking eyes with every Fighter who stood in the hallway.

The air was filled with anger, bitterness, and hatred.

It was all directed at her.

One Fighter clenched his fists. "You'll pay for this." He took a step closer, advancing at her.

Other Fighters followed his lead, approaching her with

fisted hands.

Jade gasped, backing away.

Silver and Wind were suddenly in front of her, blocking the Fighters from reaching her.

"If you hurt her, you'll hurt Nightmare. He'll never forgive you. Remember that," Wind said.

"He doesn't want a bound one, especially not *her*," a black-haired Fighter hissed.

"That doesn't matter anymore, now does it? What's done is done."

"Get back to what you were doing," Silver rose his voice. "We will handle it from now on, and if anyone interferes, he'll be locked up. Got it?"

She spotted Phoenix among the Fighters. He didn't seem as angry as the others. Instead, she saw worry and a pinch of fear in his eyes.

Did he worry she'd ruin everything now?

The bond might not be sealed yet, but once the process was initiated, there was no going back.

She *was* Nightmare's bound one now, and as his bound one, she had *almost* complete power over him.

A cyborg would do anything to please his bound one, to make sure she was happy and satisfied.

His whole existence was meaningless without her. The cyborg would die for his bound one. He'd sacrifice his life to protect the woman who loved him.

She saw it now.

Every single Fighter worried she'd tell Nightmare to turn

himself in, and that he'd do it without a thought.

Only because she asked him to.

It was written on all their faces.

Jade's chest tightened.

There was only one thing to do.

She placed her hands on Silver's and Wind's shoulders, drawing their attention, but her gaze was set on the group of Fighters in front of them, the Fighters they were protecting her from.

She inhaled with a shaky breath, and walked by Silver and Wind, approaching the Fighters.

Silver grabbed her arm. "What're you doing? They're ready to kill you."

Gently, but firmly, Jade pushed his hand away, her gaze still set on the Fighters. "I know what you're all thinking. I know you worry about what I'll do, now that Nightmare's bound to me." Her breath stuttered. Saying it was more difficult than she'd ever imagined.

She still couldn't believe it herself. It was still so fresh.

"But I give you my word. I will not let him down, or you."

No one seemed impressed.

"And how can we trust that?" Phoenix asked.

"Because my eyes have been opened. I see now why you never turned to me. Why you chose to push my help away. Your actions didn't make much sense before, but they do now. I still know very little, but even if a few words have been spoken, I'm starting to understand the bigger picture."

No one moved.

"You expect us to believe you?" a Fighter asked.

Jade shook her head. "No, but I hope you'll give me a chance."

They exchanged gazes for a long and silent moment.

Everyone still looked tense, but the anger washed slowly away.

One Fighter finally took a step forward, almost invading her personal space, but she stood her ground.

Showing fear would be a huge mistake.

"We'll be watching you," he said baring his teeth, and speaking for the whole group. He turned and left, the others followed him.

Only Celise, Silver, Faye, and Wind remained.

The hallway became quiet and empty.

"Tell us what happened," Celise said, looking Jade straight in the eyes. Her voice was calm, but the determination was unmistakable. She wasn't asking, she was demanding.

Her lips twitched. "You've changed so much over these last few weeks. You seem so much stronger."

"A lot of things have happened the last few weeks."

She nodded. "They sure have." Jade sighed; the ache in her chest was just as present now as it had been when his eyes had flashed. "Nightmare threatened to kill me if I didn't reveal where the poison was hiding in the bond's code. When I couldn't show him, he started counting to five."

The sound from the gun still echoed in her head.

"We heard the shot," Wind said.

"I figured."

"You didn't reveal it to him?" Celise asked.

She shot her a dark glare. "I don't *know* anything about a poison. How many times do I have to tell you that? I was completely unaware, until you all mentioned it, and I believe Nightmare has finally understood that."

"Why do you think that?" Wind asked.

"He fired the gun, didn't he? He said he'd count to five, and if I didn't give him the answer, before he'd reached five, he'd fire it."

Silver didn't look convinced. "Then what?"

Jade cleared her throat. "We ... argued ... and his eyes flashed."

Faye frowned. "How can his eyes flash without you touching him?"

"I don't know." That was a question echoing in her mind. It was unbelievable, *not possible*, and yet, it'd happened.

A loud roar sounded down the hallway, making everyone jump.

"We don't have time for this," Celise's eyes were wide as she looked in the direction the yell had come from. "He'll come for you soon." She looked at Jade. "Are you willing to seal the bond?"

She tensed. Sealing the bond meant sex, a lot of sex.

Jade had never been intimate with a cyborg for all the obvious reasons, but she knew very well how intense a bonding was, and a bonding with Nightmare would be no different.

It also meant she'd never be able to leave this place.

Hers and Nightmare's fates would be locked together forever.

One part of her loved that thought, but another already felt the misery that would increase with each day from being in his presence.

"I wish there were another way," her colleague said.

Jade gave her an understanding smile. "Me too."

"You love him."

She nodded. "Yes, but that will never be enough."

Their expressions were almost identical.

They pitied her.

Silver and Faye had gone through something similar recently. Things had turned out fine for them, but that didn't mean it would turn out fine for her and Nightmare.

They were two completely different people compared to Faye and Silver, but there was no other way.

Her heart longed for Nightmare, even if it meant being with him would destroy her.

"I'm ready."

CHAPTER 18

Nightmare stopped after running what felt like hours—or forever. He leaned against the wall, and his lungs burned. His breathing came fast, and sweat ran down his cheek. His whole body ached, but deep down, this was a good pain, because it helped mask what was going on within him.

The bond.

It'd been initiated.

The first flash had taken place.

How the heck did that happen?

He groaned, trying to push back the desperation that rose in his chest from all the new emotions that had awakened within him.

Love.

Desire.

… Lust.

He tore at his shirt as the image of Jade's sweet face

entered his mind. It triggered his desire even more, making it tight in his pants.

Another drop of sweat ran down his cheek, but this one from the overpowering need that showered him.

Nightmare closed his eyes, rested his head back, and moaned. His mouth hung half open. It'd been a long time since he felt this intense need.

He'd felt it when Carolyn had bound him to her.

His eyes shot open, staring ahead.

Carolyn.

Nightmare cringed on the inside.

The night before he'd escaped, his brothers were already dead, he'd been chained to the floor, naked, in the middle of her office.

She'd been working on something, ignoring him, and doctors had come and gone, leaving papers, stopping by for a chat.

Many of them had stopped for a look, especially the female doctors.

The humiliation had been awful, but that hadn't been the first time. Carolyn did it to punish him for trying to go against her.

Once she'd been done with her work, she'd taken the humiliation to the next level, allowing another female doctor touch him.

There was no greater pain for a cyborg than being touched by a woman that wasn't his bound one.

His bond had gone completely haywire, and the woman

had taken her time caressing him, touching him places she shouldn't.

Nightmare had eventually passed out.

He'd awoken alone in her office, still lying on the floor, but untied. The chains had laid next to him with a key close by.

Someone had released him.

To this day, he had no idea who'd done it, but an alarm had gone off shortly after.

He'd managed to escape that night.

Carolyn had died some time later, and here he was now, struggling with this surreal bond coming alive within him. Again. It was still going strong, pleading him to go back to Jade, to seal it.

His body trembled.

It took every last little inch of him to not do it.

"Nightmare?"

He flinched.

Blaze's worried voice was behind him. Thankfully, no one else was with him.

Concern lingered in the medic's red shining eyes. "You look like shit."

"Thanks."

"I thought about asking how you're doing, but I see now I don't need to." He straightened his back. "Do you want me to do something for you?"

Nightmare's lips twitched. In a way, it felt nice to have someone worried about him. He'd never had that, until the

Fighters started to enter his life. Now, they were like a family who cared about each other, more or less. "Like what?"

"I can sedate you. That will give us time to figure out what to do."

"I appreciate the gesture, but there's nothing you *can* do to stop this from …" He let out a desperate groan. "I never in a million years thought it would end like this."

"Can you tell me what happened?"

"My eyes fucking flashed." He tried to keep his voice calm, but it was difficult to control the anger from taking over. He felt tricked, fooled. "I didn't even touch her. I never imagined the bond would go to this extent. I was convinced the bond needed an intimate touch to be initiated."

"It *does* need an intimate touch," Blaze said, sounding certain.

He shot him a look. "Are you sure?"

The medic nodded. "Yes, something else must've triggered the bond. What happened before your eyes flashed?"

He frowned and fisted his hands. "She told me she loves me."

The other cyborg's eyes widened. "She decided to tell you?"

Nightmare deepened his frown, surprise filling him. "You mean you knew?"

Blaze cleared his throat. "We figured it out when you were unconscious. The way she took care of you …" He shook his head.

His chest tightened, but he needed to hear this. "What

did she do?"

The medic inhaled, as if preparing himself. "I doubted it at first, thought she was acting, but with each passing day, it became obvious her feelings were real. She stayed by your side every waking hour, making sure you were taken care of, that nothing was missing, checking you regularly. She even slept on the chair next to your bed." He licked his lips. "Nightmare, she would've died for you."

He stared at his friend, speechless. His bond, on the other hand, was thrilled.

It poked at him, increased his blood pressure, made his body tremble even more.

Run to her!

Seal the bond!

He took a step in her direction but stopped when he realized what he was doing. Nightmare let out a frustrated growl. He'd been able to control the bond for over forty years.

He wouldn't let it win now.

He stared down the hallway, in the direction Jade was, with shaky knees and fast breaths.

It was a fight he'd soon lose.

Nightmare felt it in his whole body.

Tired.

So damn tired.

After all this time, after everything he'd been through, the exhaustion finally took over. He swayed on his feet when dizziness hit.

Too much.

His body had had enough.

Blaze grabbed his arm, preventing him from falling. "Are you all right?"

"I'm just so damn fed up with everything." His gaze lingered down the hallway again.

He was tired of fighting. Tired of struggling but protesting wouldn't make things better. Silver almost died from his bond to Faye, and the same thing would happen to him if he denied it what it wanted.

He tried to tell himself things would be different this time.

Jade *wasn't* Carolyn. She'd never hurt him like that. She'd love him, care for him … die for him.

She already loved him.

He took another step in her direction.

"You believe her," Blaze said.

Nightmare nodded, taking a third step, then a fourth … and kept walking.

The medic cyborg remained by his side.

"I've no idea if her confession triggered the bond, but I don't think so. What I *do* think is I must return to her." He placed his hand on his chest. "I'm starting to feel her *here*. The bond is demanding her, starting to love her."

It grew, fast, with determination, and with every step he took, it spiked in his heart. Filling him with desire, raw need, making him see her smiling face in front of him again.

Nightmare let out a silent cry.

Desperation filled him.

The feelings weren't real.

They weren't his, and yet, they led him back to her. Soon, he'd be nothing more but a mindless beast, unable to control himself, only after one thing.

Jade.

He groaned but kept walking, stumbling forward, staring ahead down the long hallway.

It grew again, intensified, turning into pain. It was too much, too fast. He wasn't far from hyperventilating.

How the hell had Silver done it? It took days before Faye gave him his second flash.

Blaze followed him. He didn't say anything, but Nightmare didn't miss the medic's tense expression or the sorrow in his eyes.

The bond screamed within Nightmare. No, it roared.

The pain rose to new levels.

If he didn't find Jade soon, it'd tear him apart, drive him crazy with a need and desire so strong it'd kill him.

She was his only hope.

He let out another cry. This was almost impossible to handle. The emotions the bond threw at him just continued growing, evolving, getting stronger and stronger, demanding her.

He needed to be in her arms, now. He needed the passion he'd only find in her embrace. If not, the bond would soon break him, it would devour him, it would drive him crazy, it would—

… stop?

Nightmare haltered.

What was *this*?

Blaze approached him. "What is it?" He looked him over.

"It stopped."

The medic blinked. "What?"

Nightmare pressed his hand to his chest. He remained still and quiet for a long moment as his breathing calmed. "The pain, it's gone. The mad desire to bond with Jade is … under control."

Blaze frowned. "What're you talking about?"

Nightmare frowned, too. He had no answer but couldn't be more thankful. He let out a shaky breath and pressed his hand harder against his chest.

There was something there.

Deep down.

A … feeling.

A beautiful and cozy feeling. It made him see Jade in front of him again, and this time, he smiled.

He recognized it. It was that feeling he'd pushed aside for so many years, that feeling that made his heart flutter every time he saw her. Strangely enough, it was now pushing the bond away, no, not pushing, dominating it.

How was that even possible?

The feeling wrapped itself around him, calming him, soothing him, but the bond demanded closure. It still needed to be sealed, but it could no longer hurt him, because of that … feeling.

That sweet, sweet feeling.

He gasped.

Could it be?

Could it *really* be …?

True love?

Love that *hadn't* been forced upon him?

Love that had awakened all on its own?

No, a cyborg couldn't fall in love on his own … right?

Nightmare shook his head. How could he be sure anymore?

He started walking again.

Jade.

He needed her.

The new sensations made him almost burst out in laughter.

He'd never felt anything like this with Carolyn. He'd been in love with her, but only because the bond had forced him to love her. Rejecting it had hurt like hell, but he'd done it anyway, but this time … rejecting it was not on his list.

Not anymore.

He felt the love the bond was awakening within him, but he also felt the love that had always been there.

A love he'd barely been aware of, until now.

And it felt so damn good!

He also had more control than he'd expected.

Why? That was … unheard of.

Nightmare held back the moan that wanted to escape his lips.

Faye and Silver wouldn't appreciate it as he approached them. They were the only ones left near Jade's room that he'd ruined.

"Where's Jade?"

They stared at him with wide eyes.

"Are you in control?" Silver asked.

"So far, but I need to go to her. Where is she?"

The cyborg clenched his lips, the unspoken words shone in his eyes.

"Let's save the discussions for later," he told him as frustration in his body rose. He didn't have time for this.

"Celise and Wind took her to your room. She's waiting for you," Faye said.

Nightmare took off, leaving them and Blaze behind.

CHAPTER 19

Nightmare's room was nice. It was twice as big as the room she'd been assigned to. There was a wide king-sized bed, a wardrobe with glass doors, a well-organized desk, and plants to fill out the windowless walls.

The room had taken her by surprise. She hadn't expected him to be this organized. Honestly, Jade had no idea what she'd expected. Until just a few days ago, she had no clue what the Fighters lives were like.

She'd imagined them living somewhere in the forest, maybe in some abandoned house, like the one they'd taken Shade to when they'd tried to remove his bond.

It amazed her how he'd managed to put all this together. This whole place. Jade had no idea how far below the ground they were, but it was obvious every tiny part of it had been well thought out. After all, he'd had about forty years to fix it, and she would've loved to know how he did it.

But there was no time for that. He'd show up any minute, and she barely dared to imagine what state he'd be in; probably not the best.

The bond would rule him, he'd be furious, angry with her, but he'd also have no choice.

Eventually, he'd have to give in.

If he didn't, he'd die.

The need and desire would slowly drive him crazy, completely take over his thoughts, and press his body to unimaginable heights. The stress alone would be able to take out his heart.

Jade sat on the bed, staring at the floor.

Her life, as she knew it, was over.

She'd hoped to escape this place somehow, but there was no escaping *this*.

Nightmare's fate and life were now literally in her hands.

The door flung open and Nightmare entered.

Jade met his gaze and winced.

He seemed to be in control, which was surprising, but his tension was clear. His gaze was focused on her, his teeth clenched, but then there was that hint of complete surrender.

A pinch of fatigue radiated from him.

Her chest tightened. It hurt to see him like this. She barely dared to imagine what was going on inside his head.

Once again, he was being bound to the CEO of MedAct, but she still knew so little about what he'd been through. She only knew the things she'd read in his files, and those things had mostly been medical and cold.

He'd always been called "the subject." His name had been Zero, to indicate he'd been the first cyborg, but he'd been viewed as nothing more but a thing.

Carolyn hadn't stated that straight out, but it'd been there, between the lines.

Jade's hand trembled when she placed it against his fit chest.

The shine in his eyes was intense. The bond waited for the next flash.

His black hair was on all ends, and he'd even wounded his hand from going crazy on all the furniture, but he didn't seem to care.

She swallowed, waiting for him to take the first step.

"She never loved me," he said with a low voice.

"I know. I figured that much from her files."

Nightmare remained silent for a moment. "She hurt me."

The tension in her chest grew. Something told her she wasn't going to like hearing this. "How?"

"In many different ways. Her favorite thing was chaining me to her office floor naked and beating me with a stick until I had no skin left. Then she'd fuck me and once she was done, she'd leave me lying for hours."

Jade gasped, and a raw feeling of disgust followed, filling every part of her body, making her nauseas. Her jaw remained open as the image of him chained to the floor crossed her mind. The files never mentioned that, but she

167

didn't doubt him. Not anymore. "I will never do that to you."

"I don't believe you." He still seemed calm, even if the bond had to be going havoc within him.

Maybe he was able to control the need somehow.

"I swear to you. I've never cared about anyone the way I care about you."

Nightmare tilted his head, studying her. "Why did you never tell me how you feel?"

She didn't need to ask him what he meant. "Because, in your eyes, I was the enemy."

"Not in the beginning. I had hopes for you, but when you continued creating cyborgs with the bond, you turned me away from you."

A pinch of hate awakened within her, but not toward him, toward herself. "I didn't know."

He took a deep breath, and that incredible chest rose and fell. "*That* I do believe. Somehow, Carolyn manipulated everyone, even the doctors that weren't close to her, that the bond was necessary for the cyborgs to live."

Jade nodded. "That's what the whole world believes."

"It's a lie."

She nodded again. "I understand that now."

His eyes narrowed. "So, you believe me?"

"Yes. There's no reason for you to lie, not after everything I've seen these last few days."

"Good." He took a step closer, entered her personal space, and cupped her cheeks.

Jade's heart took off. Nervousness flittered inside her because of what was coming.

Besides, he'd never looked at her the way he did now.

Nightmare's gaze was filled with desire, longing, and … love. It was as if it was awakening right in front of her.

As if he really wanted this.

That couldn't be right, right?

"I'm so sorry," she said with a shaky voice.

"For what?" His finger gently caressed her cheek.

"For giving you no choice. I never wanted this. I wanted you to come to me voluntarily."

His lips twitched. "Don't worry about it. It wasn't your fault."

She blinked.

What did that mean? Did he know why his eyes flashed? Had he figured it out? Was that why he was so calm?

She'd expected a crazy look, a desperate need, and heavy breathing; not this control he was showing. It was weird. A newly bound cyborg didn't usually behave like this.

Jade opened her mouth to ask what he meant, but before she got the chance, Nightmare pressed his lips to hers.

A shockwave of heat traveled through her, making her knees weak.

How many times hadn't she dreamt about this? How many times had she imagined this?

She'd lost count, but it wasn't important.

The kiss was gentle, careful, as if he was testing her.

She wanted to wrap her arms around him, to press

herself closer, and feel the heat of his body against hers, but she didn't move.

What if he reacted badly? What if he pushed her away despite the active bond?

After what he'd just told her, he probably would.

Jade had to prove she was nothing like Carolyn. Starting with letting him be in control.

She took off the belt to her jeans and handed it to him.

Nightmare frowned. "What's this?"

"Tie me up. I want you to be in control." Damn, that was difficult to say. She was a control freak after all, used to be the one in the leader position, and here she was, willingly giving it away.

His eyes went wide, then he grinned. "You'd let me do that?"

She swallowed but nodded. "If you need it."

"It's tempting, but I see your fear. It's not necessary, but you're not allowed to ride me."

Jade nodded again.

That was understandable.

Nightmare suddenly swayed on his feet.

She grabbed his arm, but if he fell, she wouldn't be able to hold him up. He was too tall and too heavy. He towered over her with his large and wide frame. "Are you all right?"

He took a deep but shaky breath. "It's the bond." Nightmare placed his hand on his chest. "It's demanding my attention." The already intense shine in his eyes intensified and a loud moan left his mouth, and yet ...

"You seem unusually calm about this. I've seen how Fighters react once the bond is initiated, and they almost lose control. You, on the other hand, are still standing there, in front of me, not touching me."

Should she be insulted?

His lips twitched again. "You've no idea how much I want to touch you and throw you on the bed to seal the bond, but I'm able to control it to some extent to stop it from turning me into a mindless bastard."

Jade frowned. "How do you do that?"

He shook his head as if he was trying to shake something off. Apparently, it was starting to get to him. "I'll tell you later."

She opened her mouth to protest. She wanted to know now, but when he threw off his shirt, she froze and stared at the masterpiece in front of her. She'd already seen him half naked, but this was different.

There wasn't an inch of fat on his upper body. His chest muscles were defined and prominent, and the six-pack was impossible to miss. Even the sight of his smooth and hairless skin made her lower parts clench and heat up.

"I like the effect I have on you," Nightmare said.

She cleared her throat. "Well, that's because ... because ..."

"Because you love me."

Her eyes shot to his. The gentle smile he wore as he placed her hand against his chest made her breath stutter, and in his gaze, there was love.

So much love.

He looked at her as if he'd never seen anything more beautiful. He devoured her, seemed to drown in her eyes, as he placed his hand against her cheek.

Admiration was there instead, mixed with complete devotion, and desire. The hate, the anger, and the despair was gone.

Nightmare had completely given in to the bond.

Tears gathered behind her eyes, but she managed to hold them back. He didn't need her pity.

Instead, she wrapped her arms around him and pressed her face against his chest.

To her surprise, he wrapped his arms around her too.

"You've no idea how much I've longed for this moment." She didn't want to hide the truth anymore.

Nightmare chuckled. "You're longing is over. I'm yours."

CHAPTER 20

There was a question in her eyes. "Just like that?"

He wanted to tell her yes, but she'd have a hard time believing it. "Undress," he told her instead with a gentle voice.

She inhaled a deep and shaky breath, but she obeyed.

Nightmare stood still and watched her unbutton her shirt with trembling fingers. The nervousness lingering in her eyes didn't pass him by, but there was also a pinch of anticipation and excitement.

This had to be a huge moment for her, to finally be touched by the one whom she'd loved for so long.

He still had a hard time grasping it, and as he watched her, he ran every memory through his mind, every memory of them together.

Every argument, every wild discussion, every disagreement, and every frustrating question that'd led them further and further apart.

His hate had grown, but her hate had never been there.

Nightmare saw it now.

She'd been angry, yes, but the hate he'd always believed to be there had all been in his head.

It'd always just been a strong frustration from her side, a desperation that'd made her go crazy whenever they'd communicated.

He'd been blind.

His past had blinded him.

Unintentionally, he'd compared her to Carolyn from the start, expecting Jade to be the same, and when she continued implanting the bond into newborn cyborgs, he'd seen her as a new Carolyn.

Because of that bitch, Nightmare had pushed his own feelings for Jade aside, allowing hate to rule, but now, he knew better.

He understood now.

He'd loved her from the start.

And it was a love *not* ruled by the bond.

It was like a slap to the face … and he liked it.

The bond wasn't in control. It really wasn't in control!

His feelings had developed first, long before the first flash had even happened, stopping the bond from taking over. Sure, it still messed with him, and it still needed the three flashes, but at least he wouldn't throw himself at her like some crazed maniac.

If he'd known this sooner, his life would've been different, but he'd never even considered a cyborg could fall in love without the help of the bond.

He, and every Fighter with him, had always been completely focused on the bond.

Threatening her with the gun, seeing her tears, had been so difficult!

Taking her to the kitchen had been difficult too, but he'd still done it, because hate and frustration had been the most powerful feeling.

Nightmare swallowed when her bra fell to the floor, and it jarred him back into the room—into the present.

Jade avoided his gaze and pink spots appeared on her cheeks. Then, she dared to meet his eyes, dropping her hands to her sides. A shy smile spread on her lips.

The sight of her full breasts shot his blood pressure high. All he could do was stare as further breaths got stuck in his throat. The temptation to touch her smooth golden skin was almost overwhelming.

The sweet feeling filled him again, that feeling that made him feel so cozy and fluffy on the inside just from *looking* at her.

Nightmare chuckled, earning a surprised look from her.

Her eyes narrowed. "You seem way too happy, considering you've just wracked an entire room."

"I *am* happy." He laid her on the bed.

"Why?"

"I'll tell you later." He unbuttoned his pants, and seconds later, Nightmare stood naked in front of her. He managed to hold eye contact for a moment, but when Jade's curiosity took over, her gaze trailed lower.

A gasp left her mouth as she visually inspected his private area. "You sure don't go with the standard cyborg size."

He grinned. "I know." Nightmare leaned over her. The bond demanded him to start, to rip the rest of Jade's clothes off, and take her fast and hard, but he pressed his lips together. "When was the last time you did this?"

She cleared her throat. "About sixteen years ago."

He frowned.

Jade gave him another shy smile. "Ever since you entered my life, you've been the only one on my mind. I couldn't stomach the touch of another man, and besides, my work occupied me."

The love his heart carried for her intensified. It sang inside his chest the sweetest love song, but on the outside, surprise dominated.

"I see you didn't expect that answer," she said.

"No, I didn't. You've amazed me a lot today."

She blinked. "I have?"

"More than you can imagine."

Jade frowned. "I don't understand. I bound you to me, I saw you go crazy, I saw your despair and fear, your hate, but now, you—"

He placed a finger over her mouth. "Enough talking." He grabbed her hands and placed them over her head before going for a nipple.

The hunger within him grew. Objecting against the

bond had reached its peak. He had no other option but to give in, allow it to bind him to Jade for life … and he didn't mind a bit.

Another chuckle left him. She tensed from surprise underneath him, but when Nightmare swirled his tongue around her sensitive skin a loud gasp left her lips.

Her soft flesh was like an aphrodisiac. It transported his mind to a blissful place.

He closed his eyes, didn't want to move away from the smooth feeling of her warm body against his. He explored every part of her he could reach, licking, teasing, yearning for more, and earned one shaky gasp after another in reward.

Never in his wildest dreams had Nightmare imagined it could feel like this. The only experience he had was with Carolyn, and he didn't want to remember.

The thought of touching a woman ever again after all that had made his stomach turn, but not anymore, not when it came to Jade. He'd fallen in love with her on his own, of his own free will, and it made him laugh out loud again.

Jade looked up with wide eyes. "You're laughing?"

"Don't worry about it." Nightmare went for her lips and felt her relax under his touch as he finished undressing her between kisses and impatient caresses.

The silent gasps and moans that left her mouth spiked his desire and watching her tremor from his touch was beyond pleasing.

He took his time, not stopping the fog from taking over.

Desire burned like wildfire. The combination from his own feelings and the bond's was an empowering cocktail.

Nightmare didn't care that Jade pulled his hair or dug her nails into his skin between two trembling gasps. It was a pain he welcomed. It made him hurry more. "I feel so good. It's a rush like I've never felt before."

She gave him an uncertain but passion filled smile. "Nightmare …"

"Later. I need you."

Jade parted her legs, and he almost forgot to breathe. She was inviting him in, reaching for him.

He wanted to continue exploring her, but the blinding blazes in his body were too much to handle.

Nightmare met her gaze to ensure she was ready.

Jade gave him a shaky nod.

That was all he needed as he reached for his cock and guided himself to her.

Her cheeks flushed and her eyes widened as he slowly entered her.

He let out a loud groan when her walls clasped around him. His limbs jittered, but he held back the need to start pumping fast and hard.

She needed time to adapt.

The last thing he wanted was to cause her pain.

Funny.

Just a few hours ago, he'd been ready to do just that—at least emotional pain, and he had.

She looked just as shocked as he felt.

The feeling was so different from what he remembered.

He'd also never been in this position, and that made his body tremble even more. "Jade," he whispered.

Jade wrapped her arms and legs around him. "I know."

Nightmare was unable to say anything more, he drowned in her world instead. The heat from her warmth was the most amazing sensation. He embraced her, desperately trying to get closer as he started thrusting.

She was becoming his entire universe, and with each powerful drive, the need to protect her, to love her, grew stronger. It wrapped itself around his heart like a chain that would never let go.

He was beyond the point of return. There was no going back, and despite everything that'd happened just hours ago, he didn't want to.

The second flash came without a warning. He managed to turn his head away just in time to not blind her.

A shout left his mouth as the feelings the bond awakened within him intensified, making his head spin.

The bond had been accepted.

He was hers now.

He'd do anything for her now.

Nightmare wanted it.

He wanted it all.

His hips moved with determination and he rested his head against her shoulder.

Her moans and sounds of passion spiked his own. She took everything he gave, didn't protest against the raw passion he showered her with.

Jade's breathing came faster and faster, and seconds later he felt her tighten around him as she screamed out her pleasure.

Her body quivered beneath him.

How could this kind of pleasure even exist? It made him forget who he was, what'd led to this, and just seek himself higher and higher.

He raised his upper body, threw his head back, and with everything he had, he reached for the next level.

Nightmare's body quaked, sweat broke out on his forehead and chest, his whole world spun, but none of that mattered.

The need grew. The feeling intense, too intense …

His eyes heated again.

The third flash was near, and the heat became stronger with each determined thrust.

So close …

Closer, and closer …

And …

Nightmare roared. His body exploded in a haze of lust and pleasure. He felt the third and final flash run through him, and for a short second, he thought his head would burst.

After what felt like forever, he collapsed on top of Jade.

The room fell into silence.

Her arms lay lazily on his back, and her warm breath teased his ear.

The bond was awake.

It was pleased and it purred inside his heart. However, it didn't control him.

It was different this time.

The bond literally had no control over him.

He felt everything it wanted him to feel—love, passion, desire, a need to protect Jade, but he could silence those feelings. He could push the bond aside and only allow his true feelings to surface.

Nightmare burst out into another bout of laughter.

This was like re-discovering the wheel all over again.

She grabbed his face and studied him with wide eyes. "You're laughing again?"

"You've no idea how good it feels right now."

She frowned. "I don't understand."

Nightmare pressed his lips to hers. Her confusion still lingered in the air, but he wasn't ready to share his new discovery, but he could share the love he felt.

He really loved her.

And, he did for real.

CHAPTER 21

Last night had been amazing, but Nightmare's complete turnaround was beyond confusing.

He'd gone from ruining the room she'd been kept in with pure rage, to laugh and be seemingly happy like never before. His behavior didn't make sense.

Had he accepted the bond, just like that?

No, there had to be something else, but what?

And why did he refuse to tell her?

Jade had expected him to despise her by now.

Her frustration spiked, but she didn't let it set. Instead, she focused on the long white corridor in front of her. There were other things she had to concentrate on right now.

Nightmare held her hand as they walked toward the gathering room. He seemed just as tense as she was, and it didn't surprise her.

They were about to face all the angry Fighters.

Everything still felt surreal, and Jade would need an adjustment period to get used to the thought of being Nightmare's bound one, but that was reality now.

There was no way out for neither of them.

They could only move forward.

It was obvious, even if it was a little bit weird, that he was doing exactly that.

If he could, then so could she.

A pinch of joy hit her chest. Despite all the things that didn't make sense, she wasn't alone anymore.

Jade straightened her back when she spotted an open double door ahead. A tremor went through her when male voices reached her ears.

The Fighters were already waiting, but she wouldn't let them scare her.

This was her home now, and she had to find a way to make them trust her.

All these years, she'd believed a broken bond had made the Fighters dangerous, but it was society that made them that way.

Because no one had ever listened to them.

Every single cyborg who'd lost his bound one had known the truth, but the world had turned a deaf ear. They'd been painted as crazy, dangerous, and unpredictable.

Jade straightened her back even more.

She *was* the CEO of MedAct, and she *would* find out what was going on behind the scenes. If the company hid things from her, all hell would break loose. She'd make sure of it.

Nightmare led her closer, and a few steps later, they stood in the doorway of a huge clean room in white. There were several sofas, a television, a pool table, and plenty of desks with computers.

The room was also filled with people.

Everyone was there, glaring in her and Nightmare's direction. Only a few looked worried; especially Celise.

Nightmare's grip of her hand tightened as they entered the room.

A heavy silence lingered in the air.

The Fighters watched her.

They could sense the change.

"It's done," the leader said in a clear, loud voice. "She's one of us now, and I expect you to treat her well. Anyone who doesn't, will be thrown out."

Blaze took a step forward. "Are you all right?"

Nightmare nodded. "I've never felt better."

Silver crossed his arms over his chest. "It's the bond talking."

He took a deep breath and scanned the room. "The bond doesn't control me." His voice was louder. Clearer.

A sudden wince went through the room, and for a long moment, no one moved.

Everyone stared at Nightmare with matched expressions; deep frowns and creased brows. Whispering voices came from different corners.

"What do you mean?" Jade was just as baffled.

Had she heard right?

"Exactly what I said," he told her, then turned to everyone again. "The bond does *not* control me. I felt it complete its cycle with the three flashes, but it never gained control over me." He went silent for a while, allowing his words to sink in. "I feel everything it wants me to feel, but I can *choose* to ignore it." His gaze returned to her. "I will also live if something happens to you. I will not die with you."

Wide eyes and open mouths swept the room. Everyone stared at Nightmare, as if he'd grown another head on his shoulders.

Celise approached him with a scanner in her hands, determination in her eyes. "Please remove your shirt."

The Fighters' leader obeyed without a fuss.

Jade couldn't believe what she was seeing. He actually removed his shirt. A newly bound cyborg would've never done that.

Her colleague seemed just as surprised. "Isn't the bond telling you to not do it?"

"It is," he said, "but I choose not to listen."

She blinked. "How's that even possible?"

Nightmare hesitated, then gave Jade a quick look filled with secrets.

She tensed. What was that all about?

"I'm not sure," he told Celise.

Was that really the truth, or was he hiding something?

"Well, let's find out what we have here." Celise pressed the scanner against Nightmare's chest.

The room felt smaller when every Fighter crowded

closer, staring at Celise and the scanner, waiting impatiently for the answer. Their anger seemed gone. They all were more focused on the bond instead.

Of course, they were. The bond was their curse, and it was even more obvious with their reactions.

The bond truly was a poison, and the Fighters lived every day with the side effects. Jade no longer needed proof to know it was true.

She saw it everywhere.

It was written on every Fighter's face.

Celise's eyes were fixed on the scanner. "Jade, you might want to see this."

She approached and quickly went through all the numbers the device displayed. After about a minute, she met her cyborg's gaze, stunned. "The bond is blocked. It's live and active, but it's blocked."

Nightmare grinned, and shouting voices filled the room.

"What the heck is going on?" a Fighter yelled.

"What do you mean it's blocked?" another shouted.

The leader raised a hand, and everyone instantly went silent. The authority in his shining eyes was strong. No one dared to go against him. He was the Fighters' complete authority.

Jade's heart jumped. And *she* was his bound one.

"Continue, Jade," he said when everyone was quiet.

The scanner felt heavy in her hands. "It doesn't say why, but there's no doubt the bond has been blocked." She shook her head and bit her lower lip. "I'm seeing it, but I can't believe it. How did you do it? This should not be possible."

His grin widened. "This proves there's more to the bond than we first believed, doesn't it?"

She could only nod. "It does, and there's only one way to figure out what's going on."

His gaze narrowed. "What way?"

Jade took a deep breath. He wasn't going to like this. "I need to go back. The answers are at MedAct. You need to let me go."

His grin died. "You're not leaving! I won't let you."

She flinched from the power in his voice but didn't move. "If you really want to know what's going on, then you must allow me to return. I know it's not the best time to suggest such a thing, but I'm the only one who can figure it out."

"I agree with Nightmare," Blaze said. "You're not going anywhere. I still don't trust you. Just because you've become Nightmare's bound one doesn't make you trustworthy."

She clenched her fists, ready to argue, but it would only make things worse. Jade inhaled and relaxed, before looking Nightmare and Blaze in the eyes. "Look, I know you think you can't trust me, but no matter how hard it is to believe, I've always been on your side. Why do you think it's forbidden at MedAct to hurt any of you? Why do you think we know so little about you? It's because we don't *force* you to tell us, and that's all thanks to *me* making sure that law was passed."

A heavy silence filled the air.

Most Fighters looked at her with surprise in their eyes.

"You've no idea how much I've done to protect you. I've lost sleep on so many nights, just to make sure you're treated well in MedAct's care."

"You keep us imprisoned and you drug us," Silver growled.

She nodded. "Yes, but that's also the only thing we do. It's for everyone's protection and safety."

"You continued to implant the bond within every newborn cyborg," another Fighter growled.

Jade nodded again. "My education and knowledge told me it was necessary, and when Nightmare …" she gave him a side-look, "*showed* me the code, I couldn't see what was wrong with it … meaning whatever causes the poison is hidden in plain sight."

No one spoke, but every single Fighter stood with tense expressions.

"Think about it. How come no one at MedAct seems to know what you know? Why do you think no one believes you?"

Another silence greeted her.

"Because Carolyn Williams was somehow able to pull it off," she went on. "Somehow, she managed to trick every scientist at MedAct, back then up to today, that the bond is necessary for your survival. And believe me, I never suspected there was something wrong with the bond's code, and I know it *inside out*."

The silence remained when she scanned the room again, but it wasn't as heavy anymore.

Curiosity shone in many Fighters' eyes.

Even Celise, Silver, and the others seemed curious. Confused, yes, but very much curious.

She needed to tell them more, and Jade needed to be straight forward. "Ten years ago, some of MedAct's council members thought it would be a good idea to get rid of you all for good. They were afraid of you. They feared you'd destroy society as we know it, since more and more cyborgs started to join you." She swallowed when their shining eyes widened. "I fought for weeks to prevent it. It took everything I had to stop it."

"Liar," Silver growled.

Jade shot him a dark look. "You want proof? I can give you the access codes to MedAct's database, if you want. It's all there."

He licked his lips, hesitation replaced his anger.

Nightmare nodded. "That's how we'll do it. You'll give us the codes, and we'll find everything we need to know about the bond. You won't need to go there." He seemed pleased with himself.

She shook her head. "Some things Carolyn left behind are stored below ground on a private server that's not connected to the network. When I became the CEO of MedAct, I gained access to the information she left behind, but the Council told me I wouldn't find anything I didn't already know on the private server, and I believed them." She sighed. "I understand now it was a lie. The answer to how the poison works should be there."

His lips turned thin. "You're not going."

She held her frustration back. "I'm the only one who can give you the information you need."

"We'll find another way."

"It's actually not such a bad idea," Celise said.

Nightmare shot her a dark glare. "Are you crazy?"

"Think about it," the doctor said. "I know Jade. I've worked with her for many years, and I've seen the work she's done. I know everything she says is true. She really did do everything in her power to keep you all safe. She's made many enemies along the way just because she stood up for you."

Jade's lips twitched. Celise's faith in her wasn't completely gone, after all. "I've been gone for almost a week. Everyone at MedAct is probably wondering where I am."

"I doubt it," Blaze said. "Celise called in and said you were going on a vacation with her."

"Oh." *That* she hadn't expected, but that also meant no one was searching for her, and maybe, it was for the best.

Honestly, she didn't care about the company anymore, not after what she'd learned the last few days. Her entire world had changed, and all the crap behind her back pissed her off.

It was all true.

She'd been nothing more but a puppet.

She *had* to fix this.

Jade took a deep breath. Being Nightmare's bound one filled her with strength, decreased her fear.

No one would hurt her anymore. No one would dare, and if they tried, he'd break their necks.

That made things a lot easier.

She could argue her case.

"I'm the only one who can change things," she tried again. "I *need* to go back. I'm the only one who can find the answers."

"Enough!" Nightmare yelled, anger fueled him. "There's nothing you or Celise can say that will convince me to let you go. Just yesterday, you were my prisoner, and though you might not be a prisoner anymore, you are my bound one, and my reason for living is to make sure you're safe. Do I make myself clear?" He grabbed her hand. "This discussion is over!"

CHAPTER 22

Jade didn't speak, as he dragged her out of the gathering room. Instead, she watched his stern face from the side, waiting for him to calm down.

Nightmare didn't say anything either. They continued down the hallway without an obvious goal, but eventually, his steps slowed, and he stopped.

"Nightmare?" she asked quietly.

He sighed and pulled a hand through his hair. "You don't save any time, do you?" He didn't look at her.

"Because we barely have any." Making him see that he had to let her go would be a challenge. He wanted the information MedAct was hiding badly, and she could give it to him, but only she.

No one else.

His hand trembled in hers.

She placed her other hand on his arm for comfort. "Let

me show you, you *all* can trust me."

Her cyborg sighed again, this time with frustration. "It's not that."

"Then what is it?"

Nightmare remained silent for a long moment, staring ahead. His grip on her hand tightened. "Celise will go."

Jade blinked. "She doesn't have access to the private server. She'll never be able to get her hands on the information, and she won't know what to do."

Funny how things could change in a matter of a few days.

A week ago, she'd been MedAct's CEO. She still *was*, on paper, but she hadn't felt like it for days. Not since reality slapped had her in the face. Now, she was here, plotting about how to ruin MedAct, and not the slightest part of her hesitated.

However, deep down, sadness lingered. The company had been her life for fifteen years.

Did it really need to end like this?

Nightmare leaned toward her. He seemed calmer, but the pinch of frustration in his expression didn't escape her notice. "I don't want our relationship to start like this," he said, looking her deep in the eyes.

Jade swallowed hard. "What do you mean?"

"It's our first day, and you already want to leave me." Sadness traversed his shining eyes.

She flinched and held her breath. Of course. She should've known better. "I'm sorry. I didn't think it through."

"No, you didn't. You know very well what I'm experiencing right now. Yes, the bond is sealed, it doesn't control me, but I still feel everything it wants me to feel, and since the bond is fresh, those feelings are intense. All I want is to stay in bed with you for days."

Heat kissed her cheeks. "I don't mind that."

"Good, because that's where I'll keep you the nearest future." Her cyborg wrapped his arms around her and pulled her against his warm body. "I don't want to talk about MedAct, the bond, or the Fighters. I just want us, nothing else."

Her cheeks heated even more. The thought of *just them* and nothing else for a few days sounded tempting.

She'd been tense for so many years. She'd been working from the morning until late night almost every day, and the thought of letting everything go, just for a little while, was … thrilling. And yet, a question nagged from the back of her mind. "Why don't you hate me?"

She'd expected his grin to fade, but it didn't.

"Because I've had a revelation."

Jade frowned. "About what?"

Nightmare kissed her on the cheek, chuckling. "I'll tell you later." He grabbed her hand again, and they kept walking.

"You told me that last night, and you're making me just more curious. I thought you'd despise me forever when the bond initiated."

"I thought so, too, but as I was running away, I realized

why it initiated, and everything turned around. I actually couldn't be happier."

"You're not making any sense."

"I know, but trust me on this. I'm not lying, and when I'm ready to share, I'll let you know."

She held back a frustrated breath, but convincing him to tell her would lead nowhere. After all, he was just as stubborn as she was. "Where're we going?"

"Everywhere."

Jade frowned. "What?"

"I'm going to show you around so you get to know this place. I'm not going to show you the exit though, not until I'm sure you won't try to leave." Nightmare flashed a fast look, and all she could do was roll her eyes. "But, let's start with our spa."

She winced. "You have a spa?"

He chuckled. "When you have nothing else to do, you spend your time building this place. Over time, one cyborg after another joined me and helped. This used to be an underground bunker from a long-forgotten war. It was a wreck when I found it, but thankfully, many things were already in place, like electricity, water, and heat. All we had to do was freshen things up."

She squeezed his hand harder and looked forward to the tour, but then, she gazed at the scar on his throat. It was bulging and slightly pink in color. The skin around it seemed tight, but he didn't seem troubled by it. "Will you tell me about your scar?" Jade held her voice low, asking kindly.

Nightmare studied her. "Why do you want to know?"

"I know what MedAct thinks your story is. Now, I want to hear your story from you. After everything that's happened, I can't help but wonder how much of all the things I learned from MedAct was true."

Her cyborg remained silent for a while, as they walked down the hallway. The only sounds were their steps echoing against the white walls.

"It happened about forty years ago, when I escaped from MedAct. It was the best and worst night of my life, but I had to get away so that my brothers' deaths wouldn't be in vain."

"Your brothers?"

He nodded. "I was the first, but there were three more after me. Carolyn thought of them as failures, and when we rebelled, she killed them, but kept me and implanted the bond within me as punishment. I was her … 'masterpiece'." The words came out as a harsh bark. A pinch of anger boiled up in his eyes but faded fast. "She named me Zero. The others were One, Two, and Three."

Jade hugged his hand. "There're barely any files of your brothers. From what I learned, she was unable to wake them up because the bond didn't work on them. For some reason, it only worked on you."

Nightmare sighed. "That's not true."

"I understand that now."

"Forget everything MedAct taught you. Believe me, you'll do yourself a favor."

She nodded. "I'll find you the proof you need to expose all of this. I don't know how, or when, but I'll do it."

Nightmare's lips twitched. "I believe you." He kissed the back of her hand. "For so many years, I wanted you to see, to understand, but you stuck by the knowledge MedAct gave you, the knowledge that brainwashed you. I didn't know how to break through that, but I guess getting shot solved it for me. Celise and Blaze succeeded where I failed."

She snorted. "I trusted Celise. I suspected something was off, but I never in my wildest dreams thought she'd sided with the Fighters. I never took any precautions when I went to meet with her and Wind at their home, and that became my doom. Silver and Faye were also there, along with Soul, one of the cyborg soldiers. He shot me with something, and next thing I knew, I woke up here."

He chuckled. "So that was how it happened."

Jade shrugged. "I guess things turned out well in the end … even if you tried to break me a few times."

Nightmare cleared his throat. "I'm sorry about that. I was angry and unaware of my f—" He cleared his throat again. "I know better now, and I'll never hurt you again. You can trust that."

She studied him.

Their relationship had been long and complicated, but when Jade looked into his shining eyes, she knew he spoke the truth.

"I trust you."

He blinked. "You do? Despite all the things I put you through?"

"Yes. I put you through a lot, too. I wanted you to trust me, but I never listened to you. I never heard what you were trying to tell me, and that caused a lot of issues between us."

Her cyborg kissed the back of her hand again and gave her a meaningful look. "Thank you. Your trust means the world to me."

The touch of his lips on her skin shot a longing within her she didn't need right now. Jade looked away and inhaled deeply to cool down. "Tell me more of your story."

Nightmare chuckled, obviously noticing her dilemma. "I'll take care of your need soon, I promise."

The heat in her cheeks intensified when he gave her a quick kiss, but she couldn't hold back a smile.

"On the night I escaped, I ran for hours. It rained, and it was cold, not one of the best nights to escape. I had no shoes and my feet turned into a bloody mess. I'd never been outside until that night. I barely knew anything about the world, but somehow, I managed to avoid Carolyn and her band of trained idiots for a long time, until they caught me on a bridge."

Jade couldn't help but clench her fists together as pressure filled her. She could almost see his memories in front of her.

"I managed to overpower Carolyn when she got too close, but I was just as good as dead." Nightmare went silent for a while. "My only way out was jumping from the bridge, but as I did, they started shooting. A bullet hit me in the throat. It went right through, but—"

She wrapped her arms around him and held him tight.

He winced. "What're you doing?"

"I'm holding you," she said against his chest.

"I don't mind, but why now, all of a sudden?"

She gently caressed his back and felt the shiver that went through him. "Because you need it."

For a long moment, silence lingered between them. If she looked up, she would no doubt see surprise in his shining eyes, but she didn't move.

Being this close to him was like a drug she didn't want to quit with.

"Yesterday, I was ready to do anything to make you talk," he finally said in a low voice and wrapped his arms around her. "I promised Celise I wouldn't hurt you, physically, because I didn't want to jeopardize my relationship with her, but I didn't promise her anything about hurting you mentally." Nightmare took a deep breath. "But as I pushed the gun against your head, everything within me protested. There was a feeling deep down that …"

Jade looked up, her arms still wrapped around him. "That what?"

Hesitation lingered in his eyes. "That … told me it was wrong."

"Why?"

"Because it changed everything."

"What does that mean?"

Was he talking about whatever he still refused to share with her?

He pulled away from her. "Let me show you where our

spa is." He grabbed her hand and they kept walking.

Disappointment filled Jade. Was he ever going to tell her?

It was obvious he wasn't going to tell her now. She had to be patient for a bit longer. "How long did it take to build the spa?"

"Two years. Thankfully, all the plumbing was already in place, but finding everything we needed took time. I couldn't just walk into a store and buy it."

Jade chuckled. "I guess robbing places is the Fighters' specialty."

He laughed. "We sure have become good at it over the years."

Her cyborg led her through the hallways, and it was almost impossible to keep up with all the turns. There were so many closed doors on both sides, most of them probably led to empty rooms, and there were no signs on the walls that told her where she was.

She'd be lost without him.

Soon, they stood at the end of a long hallway and in front of a metal door.

Nightmare placed his palm against the plate next to it.

There was a click, and she followed him in, her body tight, when the door opened. Jade looked around and gasped.

The room was bigger than she'd expected, and completely different from the rest of the place. There were no white walls or bright ceiling lights.

Instead, she stared at a room carved from stone, with an underground pool and gentle blue light from the water, reflecting on the ceiling. The floor leading up to the pool was decorated with beautiful mosaic patterns.

Despite no natural sunlight, several sunbeds stood near the water, along with round tables big enough to fit a few drinks. A small wardrobe stood next to the wall that led out of the room. It was filled with towels and bathrobes. Next to it stood also a fridge and a small bar filled with glasses and non-alcoholic beverages.

In another corner were gurneys, and a shelf hung on the wall next to them, filled with skincare products and massage oils.

She could stare herself blind at the beauty. "Oh my." Her voice echoed against the stone walls.

Nightmare chuckled and wrapped his arms around her from behind. "This is where I spent most of my time when I found this place, but it was nothing more but a cave back then. I had clean water, and it was warm and comfy compared to the rest of the place at that time. The headquarter was a huge mess back then."

Jade nodded and placed her hands on his arms. His embrace was soothing for her stressed nerves. "Yes, it's rather warm in here."

"It comes from a hot water spring far below the ground. This is the perfect place to go to, to escape reality for a while. We'll lock the door and spend a few hours here, just you and me."

Heat sufficed her body. "I still can't believe this is happening."

He kissed her cheek. "Me neither, but here we are."

She swallowed. "Here we are." Her voice was low, but her heart pounded harder and harder. Almost hard enough for her to hear it. Jade licked her lips and took a deep breath. A pinch of tension filled her. It was difficult to get used to Nightmare's new behavior.

A small part of her still waited for him to explode and start blaming her for binding him to her.

An even smaller part couldn't help but think this was a plan to trick information out of her, but deep down, maybe she was just being paranoid.

He was *bound* to her now.

Bound!

That alone spoke plenty, even if the bond was locked away. Besides, a cyborg would never touch a woman he didn't love.

"Shall we?" His voice was way too sweet.

His hands traveled down her arms.

Goosebumps awakened when his lips grazed the skin on her neck.

He let out a pleased sound, as if he was tasting the sweetest chocolate. "I could spend forever with you in here."

Should she laugh or cry? All of this really was so surreal.

The way he acted was so different from what she knew, but she loved it. Jade loved every piece of it, and the selfish side of her wanted everything he could give.

Jade wanted to devour it like a sponge because she was starving.

Fifteen years of longing and desire was a long time. Fifteen years of denied emotions and ignored feelings felt even longer, but now, when he was here, when *they* were here, together, she wanted to take it all.

Nightmare made a movement behind her and Jade turned her head to the side. She gasped.

He was undressing!

A tremor went through her, her knees went weak. If she dared to move, they would definitely give in. Even if they'd been together already, it would take time to get used to his overpowering presence.

Especially his naked presence.

The sound of a zipper going down filled the room.

A cold wave, as if she'd been splashed by ice cold water, went through her. She didn't need to turn around to know he was naked.

Nightmare wrapped his arms around her again and rested his head against her shoulder. "Don't ever leave me," he whispered, and with a feather-light touch, caressed her arm. "You've no idea how much I need you."

His feelings didn't make sense.

His bond had somehow been locked away.

He'd said it himself; he could ignore the feelings it threw at him, that he wouldn't die with her if something happened, so why did he *need* her?

Jade had so many questions, but his sweet caresses were

a perfect distraction. She didn't want to think about all the things around them. She wanted what he'd said earlier — to get away from everything for a while.

With him.

Jade turned around and looked him in the eyes. "I've no idea what's going on, or why you need me, but I don't care about the details right now. All I know is that I need you, too." She threw off her shirt and bra, regretting it only for a split second. Getting used to this would take time.

His lips twitched and Nightmare knelt in front of her. "Let me help you with the rest." His hands reached for her pants and he unbuttoned them with slow and gentle moves. As the pants slid down her legs, he started kissing the skin that got revealed to him.

Her panties went with the pants, and a hard tremble went through her when he moved closer to her sex.

His hot breath grazed her private area, and his tongue stuck out.

He wasn't going to, was he?

Nightmare licked between her folds with a pleased groan, slowly, as if he was enjoying the best candy he'd ever tasted.

The sensation rushed through her body, and her knees gave in.

Her cyborg caught her just before her butt hit the ground, chuckling. "Are you *that* sensitive?"

Heat rushed her whole form. Her cheeks burned, and her sex ached for more. "I'm just not used to it."

"I have a challenge in front of me then." He grabbed a

big towel from one of the chairs and placed it on the floor. "Lie down."

Jade could do nothing but obey. The excitement was too great, the thought of him doing it to her too tempting.

She expected him to go slow, to lean over her, maybe kiss her first, before he'd trail down her body with kisses and caresses, but when he parted her legs and placed himself there comfortably, she almost forgot to breathe.

Jade opened her mouth to say something; what, she didn't know, but she didn't get the chance to even think before he was at her. Her loud gasp echoed against the walls when he went full in.

Nightmare didn't give her time to adapt to the feeling of his tongue against her sensitive spot. He swirled it around her clit as her body shook beneath his rough touch.

She couldn't remember it ever being this intense. She'd had a few lovers before Nightmare had entered her life, but her sex life with those guys had never been much to cheer over. None of them had touched her the way Nightmare touched her now.

With desperation, she wrapped her fingers around his hair and held on for dear life. Sweat broke out on her forehead, another quiver went through her, and she wanted to bring him even closer.

Nightmare didn't let her down.

The lust and passion rose with every lick and swirl of his tongue, forcing the feeling to grow higher and higher. There was no going back, there was no stopping the unavoidable.

It built, built, and—

Jade threw back her head and let out a loud cry as climax took over. She shook violently beneath his touch.

He didn't stop. He kept going until she couldn't take it anymore. First then did he move away. With a wide grin, he crawled up on her. "Judging by your satisfied expression, I assume you're pleased."

She gave him a smile. "I am. That was amazing."

"And it will be even more amazing soon." He stood and brought her up with him.

Her legs wobbled, but when he led her into the pool and the warm water surrounded her, it was easier to stand.

The pool wasn't deep. The water reached her chest.

More water ran down the stone wall in front of her, like from a tiny waterfall. Gentle sounds of liquid moving and dripping filled the room.

Nightmare barely gave her time to enjoy the warmth, before he was at her again, showering her with his passion and desire.

His hands explored her, lingered over the sensitive spots, and his lips roamed over her breasts and face. His kisses were the sweetest, so gentle, and caring. Determined, yes, but loving beyond words.

Yesterday, before the bond, he never would've touched her. His hate had been clear, but today, he was all over her as if he couldn't get enough.

Wonder sang deeply in her, refusing to leave. Her curiosity grew by the minute.

What'd gotten into him?

Where did all of this come from if it wasn't coming from the bond? Why didn't he hate her like she'd expected him to?

Why did it seem like he actually loved her?

Deep down, she couldn't be happier, but she needed to know what'd happened. Needed to know what had changed.

Nightmare gave her a final kiss before he turned her around. "Lean against the edge of the pool."

She snickered and did as he asked. "So this is how it's going to be?"

"This will be easier," he said as he parted her legs. "I'm much taller than you, and even if I'm strong, I doubt I'll be able to hold you for a half hour or two."

"Half an hour?" She didn't miss his grin from the corner of her eye.

"Or at least for as long as you can take me. I know we're both a little bit rusty, but you've no idea how much I need you." He started pushing in.

Jade clenched her teeth, sensations washing over her.

He was harder than she'd expected, but that only sparked her desire, and when he leaned over her, he locked her in place with his massive frame.

Nightmare started thrusting, slowly at first, then faster and faster, until he was pounding in and out of her.

The water splashed all over, but Jade didn't care. Her focus was on him and the amazing feelings he awakened within her.

Every drive built that amazing feeling; she was reaching for it again, and when it grabbed her, it did it hard, making her scream out her passion as her walls hugged him tightly.

He let out a loud grunt, then she felt his release fill her. It almost made her purr.

Her cyborg collapsed on top of her, and she melted into the edge of the pool.

They both breathed hard.

Jade remained still for a long moment, slowly recovering. "That was a fast half an hour." She chuckled.

He cleared his throat. "I was too excited."

"I figured. It's okay."

Nightmare didn't move away. Instead, he wrapped his arms around her. "Don't ever leave me, Jade." His voice was gentle.

It wasn't a demand, it was a desire.

She wanted nothing more but to stay, but the answers to the questions the Fighters so badly needed were located *at* MedAct.

She *had* to go back.

Jade had already been gone almost a week, and even if Celise reported her and herself to take a vacation, people would soon wonder what was going on if she didn't come back within a few days. "Nightmare ..." she started.

His arms tightened. "I can't let you go. The thought is tearing me apart." A sob left his lips. "You're no longer my prisoner, you're my bound one, so I need you to promise me. Promise you won't try to go back."

A heavy feeling settled over her chest. Hesitation followed, but she opened her mouth. "I … promise."

He exhaled, relaxed against her. "Thank you."

It hurt like hell on the inside because it was a promise she wouldn't be able to keep.

CHAPTER 23

Jade stared at the ceiling from where she laid in Nightmare's bed ... no, *their* bed.

He'd said that, and strangely, this place was starting to feel more and more like home.

It'd been two days since he'd brought her to the spa, and it'd been two amazing days filled with love, laughter, a lot of touching, and even more sex. She could barely remember what her life used to be like before all this.

MedAct felt so far away.

Yesterday evening, Nightmare had finally showed her around, but he didn't show her the exit.

He explained everything about the Fighter's headquarters, how the place functioned, what the Fighters did to get food and other things they needed, how everyone had a role to play, and it all amazed her.

The Fighters' lives were more organized and structured

than she'd ever imagined.

He even told her everything he knew about the bond.

The signal he'd created to block a Fighter's bond was an amazing piece of art. Jade had never heard of such a thing. She even got to see the damage the bond made to the Fighters. She'd studied the screens with a pinch of disbelief, but it'd all been there.

She'd gone over the numbers, pictures, and diagrams for hours, and at the end, she'd been able to draw one major conclusion.

It was all true.

Everything added up.

Afterward, she spent hours with Nightmare, Celise, Wind, Blaze, Silver, and Faye in the infirmary. They'd spoken about literally everything, explaining everything.

They even told her about the female cyborg program.

Why had she never heard of it?

As MedAct's CEO, she should have.

That lack of knowledge felt like another needle in everything she'd learned to trust and believe when it came to her work.

It turned everything around, and no one in the room had been able to miss her anger.

Thankfully, they'd decided to trust her, but she understood how much pressure she'd put them under.

Their fate literally lay in her hands now.

Jade would never break their trust, though.

She took a deep breath and got out of bed. The clock

said it was five a.m., but she couldn't sleep. Too much was on her mind. After everything she'd learned yesterday, it was no surprise she couldn't sleep. Processing it would take some time.

Nightmare stirred. "Where're you going?"

She put her clothes on. "To get something to drink. Go back to sleep. I'll be right back."

His head fell back on the pillow, and he was asleep before she left the room.

Jade followed the hallways to the kitchen. She *had* to go back to MedAct now. There were still so many questions that needed answers.

She stilled, staring ahead.

Funny how things had changed these past few days. She was one of the Fighters now. Sure, many of them weren't convinced about her yet, but more and more of them had started to talk to her. They tried to approach, and that was a good start.

She would do anything for them.

Even abandon MedAct.

The company wasn't what she'd thought it was. It was a lie, just like Celise had said. She saw it now.

Jade had always believed she was doing something good creating cyborgs, but she saw the dark side now, and it was all her fault.

She'd continued Carolyn's work without ever questioning it. It'd always worked, the women who'd signed up for a cyborg had been happy, the world seemed happy, too. The cyborgs had been accepted by society without much fuss.

She shook her head. Self-pity wasn't going to help.

It'd been two amazing days, but it'd also been two days that made her realize Nightmare would never let her go. He wasn't interested in trying to put together a plan to get the information from MedAct, because it was too dangerous.

She'd given him and the others access to MedAct's main servers, but the information they needed wasn't there.

It was below ground, and to get her hands on it, she needed to return to MedAct.

By now, every doctor probably wondered where she was. Over a week was a lot for her to be away, and she felt the opportunity slip them by because of Nightmare.

Nothing bad was going to happen.

She doubted anyone suspected anything, and her going to the lower levels of MedAct to check up some files, was nothing unusual.

And yet, here she was.

Unable to leave.

Because of his stubbornness.

Jade cursed as she entered the kitchen. She approached the fridge and grabbed a bottle of mineral water.

"You look rather grumpy today."

She jumped, then twisted around.

Phoenix sat by one of the tables.

She hadn't noticed him when she'd come in.

He gave her a wide grin. "Sorry, I scared you."

Jade relaxed and sat down by his table. "Why're you up so early?"

Phoenix straightened and looked her deep in the eyes. "I've been waiting for you."

Her jaw dropped. Was he kidding? Any second now, he'd surely laugh it away, but it never happened. His face remained serious. "What do you mean?"

He took a sip of his tea. "I'm going to help you escape."

Jade's jaw dropped even more, and a pinch of suspicion filled her. What was he up to?

"I've been waiting here every morning since you bound Nightmare to you, hoping you'd one day show up so we could talk without anyone hearing. Everyone is asleep right now, and we don't use guards to defend this place. It's pointless, since the ways in and out are controlled by us."

She frowned. "That sure is a long shot."

He nodded. "It is, but that was my only option. You're allowed to walk around on your own now, obviously, without anyone keeping an eye on you, but I couldn't tell you to meet me here. The last thing I needed was someone overhearing." His determination was obvious, and the strong shine in his cyborg eyes was intense.

"You already have a plan, don't you?"

He nodded. "All you have to do is say yes."

Could she really trust Phoenix? She'd saved his life twice in the past, but it didn't mean their relationship was good. "Why are you doing this?"

"Because I still owe you. I heard what you said the other day in the gathering room, but I also heard Nightmare. He'll never let you go, but you *need* to go."

214

Jade clenched her fists. "I'm the only one who can get the hands on the information you seek. Celise can't."

"And that's why I'm going to help you, but it needs to be done now, before everyone wakes up." He stood. "Follow me, or watch your chance slip away."

She winced. This was happening a little bit too fast. She hadn't even had the chance to think things through yet.

Yes, she had to go, but leaving Nightmare and the others was a dangerous risk.

Would it ruin their faith in her for good?

It was still so fragile.

Her heart pounded as she watched him go. Was leaving Nightmare really the right answer?

What if they could come up with another plan to get their hands on the information they needed?

No, there was no other way. She *had* to go.

But leaving meant breaking Nightmare's trust. He'd be angry. Who knew what he'd do if she left.

Yet, her legs carried her out from the kitchen, following Phoenix.

He looked amused, as they walked through the empty hallways. "First, you wanted nothing more but to escape, and now, you want to stay."

"I don't like doing this to Nightmare, or any of you."

He sobered. "You're not doing anything *to* us. Nightmare's blinded by his feelings for you right now. He doesn't see what needs to be done."

She frowned. "And you do?"

"I do. You must return, and you must return now, not in a few weeks. By then it will be too late."

"Aren't you afraid I'll betray you?"

The cyborg gave her a suspicious look. "I am. I am very afraid, but deep down, I trust you."

Her chest tightened. It actually *hurt* to hear he was afraid. Had any of the Fighters ever trusted her? Even the slightest?

But his trust … was almost overwhelming.

"Why? Why do you trust me?" The question almost got stuck in her throat.

His cold gaze transformed into a warm smile. "Because I choose to. I've watched you ever since you came here. You really were oblivious to the bond's true nature. That was a huge surprise to all of us; it was unbelievable. How could the CEO of MedAct *not* know?" He took a deep breath. "And yet, you didn't." Phoenix went silent for a while. "Your feelings for Nightmare were confusing at first, but they made me realize how wrong we've all been."

Jade blinked. Her heart pounded hard. "What do you mean?"

"You and Nightmare have always had a love-hate relationship. He often shared with us how he couldn't wait to get his hands on you to squeeze the life out of you, that you'd be the one to suffer for everything Carolyn did to him, but you never were the bad one. Neither were we. We've all been played. This is a game that goes deeper than any of us ever knew."

Her throat tightened, and she nodded, more to herself

than to him. "You're saying the past fifteen years could've been avoided."

"Yes. If we hadn't been blinded by Carolyn's actions, our situation, yours and ours, might've looked different today."

Her lips twitched, and a warm feeling filled her. "Thank you."

"Don't thank me yet. I'm doing this because I trust you'll do the right thing, but that doesn't mean I'm *convinced* you will."

Jade straightened her back. Determination filled every part of her body. "I won't let you, or any of the other Fighters down. I'll do my best to find out what's going on behind our backs, but what'll happen to you once I'm gone? Nightmare will never forgive you."

Phoenix's lips turned thin. "Just make sure you'll get your hands on that information. I'll deal with Nightmare."

They stopped in front of a wide door.

The cyborg placed his hand against the plate next to it. A second later, it clicked, and the door opened.

Jade followed him and found herself inside a huge underground parking lot. There were vans, cars, and several motorcycles. "Oh, wow. I didn't expect this."

"We've had forty years to fix this place, you know. When we don't rest, we build our home."

She nodded. "You sure aren't the messy and dirty cyborgs the media makes you out to be."

"The dirty appearance is a disguise. We use it when it's needed, to confuse the world. We don't want people to know what we're really like, not yet."

She gave him a long look. "What will you do, when the time comes?"

"Nightmare didn't tell you?"

"I know about the bond, the female cyborg program, and so on, but I have no details to how things will go down."

"Everything depends on how things turn out, but the idea is to show everyone the real us, to invite a journalist here, and show the world who we really are."

Jade's jaw dropped. "You'd go that far?"

"The world needs to see we're not a bunch of dangerous and unpredictable cyborgs who don't know what we're doing. Every step we take is planned, organized, and that's what we want people to know, but right now, everything is chaos. We lost Heaven and three other Fighters when we went after the tank. We've tried to track them, but it's like they've just disappeared. Several of us are locked up because their minds are lost, and you've just bound Nightmare to you." Phoenix shook his head, exhaling. "It's a mess, but we'll get there."

She licked her lips. "They've been taken to XenthAid, and that's why you can't track them. That place is highly secured with an A.I that blocks out any signal that tries to get too close. I'll try to find information about them, if I can."

He smiled. "Thank you." His gaze turned to all the vehicles. "It's time for you to leave." He approached a motorcycle. "Can you drive this, or do you want a car? I recommend a motorcycle, though. It'll be easier to get in and out of town."

Jade smirked. "A motorcycle will do just fine."

CHAPTER 24

Nightmare opened his eyes and stared up at the ceiling. The room was awfully quiet, and Jade's side of the bed was empty.

An unnerving feeling filled him. She'd said she was going to the kitchen.

That had been an hour ago.

The clock on the wall displayed six a.m.

He got up, and the morning fatigue washed off him in a second, his senses heightened.

Something was wrong.

He dressed quickly. He'd never put on his clothes this fast before, and barely a minute later, Nightmare headed for the kitchen.

Blaze was there, looking newly awake, sipping on a warm cup of tea. "Good morning." He eyed Nightmare. "Didn't you sleep well?"

He clenched his fists. The feeling in his chest intensified as he looked around in the empty and quiet room. Most were still asleep at this hour. "Where's Jade?"

"She's not with you?" The medic's focus spiked.

"She said she was going to get something to drink, that was an hour ago."

That got Blaze on his feet. "I've been here for ten minutes, and I haven't seen her."

The dreadful feeling in his gut grew by the minute.

Did this mean what he thought, or was she just having a chat with someone somewhere?

Or had something happened?

Had one of the Fighters snapped like Edge had with Faye?

A cold shiver went down his spine. "I have to find her." He spun around, ready to head for the door, but halted.

Celise and Wind were in the doorway. They held hands, and Wind looked as if he was ready for anything.

Celise's eyes were still half-closed. She yawned and looked around. "Unusual to see you both up this early."

Nightmare didn't have time for morning greetings. "Have you seen Jade?"

The doctor instantly sobered, eyes wide. "No. She's mostly been with you for the last few days."

His body started to shake, but thankfully, he was able to hide it from the others. Chaos went through his mind. Something *had* happened. "Damn it." He headed for the door again, only to be forced to stop once more, when

Phoenix blocked his way.

The Fighter crossed his arms over his chest, intentionally not moving.

"Out of my way." Nightmare didn't like the calm look on the cyborg's face. It only pissed him off even more now that his nerves were spiked.

"I can move if you want but running around trying to find Jade won't do you any good. She's not here."

Nightmare's breath got stuck in his throat as a gasp went through the room. Every already triggered emotion went off like an explosion, making him tremble.

Betrayal. Disbelief. Confusion. Anger.

It all washed over him like a huge mix of turmoil.

The knowledge that she'd abandoned him grabbed ahold and refused to let go. It squeezed his chest hard, making it difficult to breathe.

Fear for her life and disappointment mixed into the disordered cocktail.

Phoenix placed his hand on Nightmare's shoulder, giving him a reassuring smile. "Relax. Jade will be back once she's done what she has to do."

He pushed his hand away. "Explain."

"Did you really expect Jade would do as you wanted? She's not a dog you can tame. She will go her own ways." He straightened his back. "Jade has gone back to MedAct to find out anything she can about the bond, but I assume you've already figured that out."

Nightmare frowned so hard it hurt. "How? I never

222

showed her the way out."

Phoenix inhaled, as if preparing himself, but his back remained straight. "I showed her."

He snapped. Pure fury made his blood boil and he slammed the cyborg against the wall. "How dare you?"

A loud gasp came from his side, and in the corner of his eye, he saw Celise's fear, but he was unable to let Phoenix go.

The Fighter didn't struggle. "I dared, because you made the wrong decision. This is our *only* chance to find out more about the bond, and the only one who can find that information is Jade. She *must* go back to MedAct. Not in a week or two, today. She's already been gone for a week, and that's long enough. Any longer and the doctors will suspect something."

"I didn't know you trusted her," Nightmare hissed.

Phoenix remained silent for seconds that felt like hours. "I don't, but I'm giving her a chance, and so should you."

Hesitation washed over him, sweeping away the worst rage in the process.

"She'll be fine," the cyborg assured him. "As long as you stay out of it, nothing will happen."

His mood darkened again. "How can you be sure?"

"Because they won't hurt one of their own, especially not their CEO, and *especially* if they aren't suspecting anything. As long as she sticks to the story that she's been on vacation with Celise, everything will be fine."

Nightmare clenched his teeth.

Phoenix was right, but his whole form vibrated from the almost overwhelming need to go after her.

He felt it in every part of his soul.

His bound one wasn't by his side, and even if the bond was locked away, he could feel its dissatisfaction.

Of course, Jade would be safe. He didn't doubt that. She'd worked at MedAct for fifteen years, and it'd been her haven … from him.

The one place he hadn't been able to go.

Although, he'd never really tried. All he'd managed was to break in through the main entrance to get his hands on the then newborn cyborg, Shade.

Nightmare had studied MedAct for years, even stolen the interior plans of the building, and managed to figure out another way in, but he'd never seen any use for it … until now.

Entering MedAct would be a death sentence.

They wouldn't even try to find a bound one for him, as they did for every Fighter they managed to catch.

No, he'd be sent to XenthAid.

The place had been a mystery, a rumor, for a long time, but now he knew where the Fighters who refused to bind themselves went.

Like Heaven and the other three who'd helped to get the tank. Unfortunately, he still didn't know where XenthAid was located. Nor did he know anything about it.

Nightmare shook his head. Somehow, they'd get them back, but right now, his focus was on Jade.

He was unnerved, and the sensation wouldn't leave him.

Phoenix *was* right, and yet, why did it feel like she was walking into a trap?

He was probably just being paranoid, but he couldn't shake the feeling. He headed for the door.

"Where do you think you're going?" Phoenix yelled after him.

Nightmare didn't answer.

Instead, he started to run.

"Shit," the cyborg said. "Nightmare, stop!"

He didn't.

Soon, he heard running footsteps behind him. He was fast, and knew where he was going.

Celise wasn't strong enough to stop him, and Wind wouldn't try because Celise was his priority.

Nightmare only had to worry about Blaze and Phoenix, but the medic wouldn't fight him; wouldn't try to stop him physically.

Phoenix, on the other hand, knew how to throw a punch.

"Don't do it!" Celise yelled behind him, desperation in her voice. "You'll make things worse. Trust that Jade will return."

He couldn't do that.

He had to go after her. There was no other option for him now. The determination had taken over. It drove him in her direction, and didn't matter how foolish this idea was.

He had to protect his bound one from the enemy.

Nightmare would risk his own life to keep her safe.

Blood pumped in his veins, as he rushed through the hallways with clear determination. The adrenalin surged through his body, making that goal stronger.

He had no control anymore.

His love for Jade overpowered him.

It made him run for his life to get to her.

He reached the garage, and quickly opened the door, managed to go through it, and close it just seconds before Phoenix caught up with him. In the last second, he turned the lock.

Nightmare leaned forward to catch his breath. He needed a second before he continued.

Someone banged on the door. "Nightmare, please, don't do this," Celise's voice came from the other side of the door.

He panted heavily as he looked for a vehicle. One of the motorcycles was missing. Had Jade taken it?

His grinned. She, who seemed like the sweetest thing with her adorable features and small frame had a strong and stubborn personality, and she could ride motorcycles as well, apparently.

"I'm sorry, Celise", he said, approaching another motorcycle. "I no longer have control over this. I must go to her."

"They'll catch you!" the doctor yelled.

"No, they won't. I'll be careful." He put on a helmet and gloves before starting the bike.

The banging became louder.

"Nightmare!" Phoenix roared.

He opened the gate doors to the garage, and seconds later, was greeted with the long tunnel that would take him to the surface.

Nightmare turned the motorcycle and drove out.

He was being stupid, but his heart didn't care.

CHAPTER 25

Jade scanned her office at MedAct. The room was wide, with big windows, allowing plenty of daylight to stream through. There wasn't much in there, only her working table, a chair, a few plants, a shelf, and file cabinet storage for paperwork. The place had a clinical and sterile feel to it.

She'd spent years in here.

Now, it felt like she'd walked into a stranger's room.

Getting from the Fighters' headquarters to MedAct had been easy.

Jade had followed the GPS, and an hour later, she was in place. If the world knew where the Fighters resided, they'd be in danger, and despite that, Phoenix had just let her go.

He'd trusted her.

She wouldn't betray that trust.

Finding her way back wouldn't be a problem. The GPS had guided her here and she'd memorized the route before deleting it from the device, just in case.

She'd parked the motorcycle in the garage and chose a spot where it wouldn't get too much attention amongst other motorcycles.

Hopefully, no one would notice a stolen bike. It was, without a doubt, stolen. Jade doubted the Fighters had bought it.

She chuckled. She was actually going to go back. This place didn't feel right anymore, not after what she'd been through.

Besides, Nightmare wasn't here.

The thought of him made her bite her bottom lip. He probably knew by now that she'd left, and there was only one way for him to react.

He'd be furious, disappointed, and heartbroken.

She could only hope he wouldn't be foolish enough to follow her. Phoenix had said he'd handle Nightmare, and she could only hope he'd had.

Her gaze turned to the computer.

Jade had to get to work. There were many things to go through, but she wouldn't find anything in her office.

The Fighters already had access to the main servers, and no one would even notice since she'd been the one to log in. The mainframe hadn't been hacked, it'd been entered via her password.

What they were *really* after wasn't available on the main servers. It was stored underground on a server that weren't connected to the main ones. It was a safety precaution.

During all these years, she'd assumed the most important information was available on the mainframe, but she knew better now.

The Council sure tricked her. They'd literally lied when she asked, fifteen years ago, if everything she needed was available on the main systems.

She should've been suspicious when they, time after time, refused her access to the private mainframe. That should've been a warning sign, but she'd trusted them, trusted their words, that nothing of importance was available there.

Jade sighed and ran a hand through her hair. "Idiot." Could she have treated it more wrong?

Carolyn had done everything in her power to hide the truth about the bond, and she'd succeeded. No one knew about the poison. There wasn't even anything suspicious in the code itself. Finding it wouldn't be easy. It was, without a doubt, behind plenty of locked doors, and she was no computer genius.

Jade was a scientist who knew how to create cyborgs, so where would she find someone who could help her break into the private server?

Who could she trust?

There was a knock on the door.

A smiling and happy Olive entered the room. Her red-blonde hair with pink and blue strands was put up in a ponytail, and beneath her doctor's coat, she was dressed in white pants and a pastel-colored shirt in pink and yellow. Even her socks and hair tie matched the outfit.

Before Jade got the chance to react, she received a tight hug that squeezed the air out of her lungs.

The tall and fit woman made her feel small, with her five feet four frame.

"Careful, before you break something I need later on."

Olive chuckled. "Sorry, I'm just happy to see you again. You've been gone for over a week. No one knew you were going on vacation. You didn't tell anyone."

She cleared her throat. "Well, it came suddenly. Celise suggested I needed time off for a few days."

"Where did you go?"

Jade winced. She'd forgotten to ask Celise what she'd said about that. "Um ... a little bit here, a little bit there."

Olive only nodded.

She exhaled silently. Her colleague didn't seem too interested in the answer, but it was obvious a question lingered on her mind.

"Did ... Soul go with you?"

Jade blinked.

Soul.

She hadn't thought of him for several days, and the sting of betrayal still sang in her heart, but she understood his actions better now. "No, why do you ask?"

Olive licked her lips. "He's gone missing. No one can find him. We've been searching everywhere, but he's not even responding to Janice's calls, and that *never* happens with a cyborg soldier. They always come running when their bound one seeks them out."

She held her breath, studying Olive. Soul was missing? He hadn't returned?

The last time she'd seen him was at Wind's and Celise's place. He'd threatened her with a gun, and later shot her with a dart dipped in a drug that'd made her pass out.

When he'd switched sides, she couldn't say, but it was obvious he'd been with the Fighters that day. Yet, she hadn't seen him among them at headquarters.

Had he been locked up like some of the Fighters?

Or had something happened?

The worry in Olive's eyes was obvious. "I kept searching when everyone else stopped. Janice doesn't even seem to care if something happened to him, and she's his bound one, for heaven's sake!" She sobbed, quickly drying away a tear before forcing a smile. "I hoped you'd know something."

Jade swallowed as the pressure in her chest rose. "I'm sorry, but I have no information. This is the first I'm hearing of this."

She'd have to ask Nightmare.

Olive exhaled, resignation shining in her eyes. "I just want to find him, you know. I loved working with him. He's always been my favorite cyborg soldier."

She placed her hand on her friend's shoulder, meeting her gaze. "We'll find him. I promise I'll do everything in my power to find him, but I need your help first."

Her colleague relaxed and smiled. "Anything."

Her lips twitched. "Good."

Was she trusting Olive too much?

Was Olive even trustworthy?

Jade nodded to herself. *Yes,* she could trust Olive. They'd had a good relationship over the ten years she'd worked for MedAct.

Everyone liked her, even the cyborg soldiers who usually were difficult to please. She had no issues being around them, while other doctors held their distance because of the cyborg soldiers' powerful presences.

Olive was responsible for them for that reason, because few dared to do what she did. She took care of them, made sure everything functioned, and if it didn't, she repaired them.

She was also a computer genius.

"What do you want me to do?" she asked.

Jade inhaled. If she'd misjudged Olive, this would turn ugly fast.

She doubted Olive knew what was going on, and if she didn't, she wouldn't believe easily.

There was no other place to start but with the truth. "I need you to hack MedAct's private server."

CHAPTER 26

Nightmare's heart thundered as he guided the motorcycle through the city. There was no other way but to go *through* to get to where he needed to go. The visor was down on his helmet, so the risk of anyone recognizing him was slim, but it still felt like everyone was staring. A shiver went down his spine when he made eye contact with an older man for a split-second.

What if someone recognized him by his body shape?

That would be a disaster.

He swallowed and continued down the road.

Nightmare hadn't been on these streets in a long time. Last time was when he'd run from MedAct to save his life, to get away from Carolyn.

So much had changed since then. Barely anything looked the same.

When they'd gone after Shade, they'd used other roads,

and everything had been planned.

Now, nothing was planned.

Yet, he couldn't stop himself from doing this, even if his head told him he'd never been this stupid. His bound one wasn't by his side. She was among the enemy, and it drove him forward.

He *had* to find her.

He *had* to make sure she was safe.

Later, he'd teach her a lesson for leaving him.

Only a mile away from the MedAct building, underground tunnels were located. They were there in case of emergency. If a fire happened, people could use them to get out, but now, he was going to use them to get *in*.

According to what he'd learned, they should lead him directly to the underground levels of MedAct, where he assumed he'd find Jade.

Phoenix had said Jade should be there, searching for Carolyn's hidden files.

He'd studied the plans of the building for years. He knew them by heart, and his good memory would help him now.

With determination, Nightmare drove the bike forward, turning onto a side street. He followed the small alleyway for a short while before he ended up on a cemented, open space between several tall buildings.

He stopped and switched off the bike, scouting the area.

It was unusually quiet, and only the dying sounds from the motorcycle's engine echoed. There was no fence, only an entrance in the middle of the open space, leading down into a tunnel.

Strange.

He'd expected the place to be guarded, but it was empty. Not even a bird was in sight. The area felt dead, as if the world itself had forgotten about it.

He scanned the walls, carefully examining every single building.

Cameras.

Of course.

He snorted.

Did they really think cameras would stop a cyborg?

Nightmare inhaled, focusing on every camera he could see, and seconds later, his mind connected with their system. Another second passed, and he came to a halt.

A defense program.

Bravo.

At least, MedAct was smart enough to protect the cameras, but they weren't smart enough to protect this area.

Didn't matter.

Taking out the defense program would be a child's play. He cleared his throat, and went to work, slowly breaking into the software that stopped him from moving forward. He made a few twists, replaced a few zeros and ones, aaannddd ...

Crash!

He felt it happen, as he disconnected himself from the now-dead cameras.

Nightmare grinned.

Idiots.

They made this way too easy.

He left the motorcycle behind and approached the door in the middle of nowhere. It was a big metal door with a warning sign in red written on it.

Entry forbidden for unauthorized personnel.

His grin darkened. Well, technically, he *was* personnel since he belonged to MedAct. He was their creation, but that was where it ended.

Nightmare pulled the door.

Locked.

Well, he would've been disappointed if it hadn't been. It would've turned MedAct into a joke.

He had a hard time taking them seriously. It didn't matter that his bound one was the present CEO of MedAct. He'd never take the company seriously. Not after what he'd learned.

Anger boiled in his veins for everything he'd been through because of them, and if Carolyn had been alive, he would've killed her.

Watching that bitch suffer as she died slipped him by, and that fueled his anger even further.

She deserved to be dead, but she should've died by his hands.

He didn't doubt that Jade didn't know anything about the bond, not anymore, but it was still beyond him how such information was not in every MedAct doctor's grasp.

How could they not know?

Nightmare took a deep breath, forcing himself to relax.

He had to focus.

He had to find Jade.

Nightmare grabbed the handle firmly and yanked. He did it a second time, then a third. Something broke on the inside of the door as it started to bulk outward.

His lips twitched. Well, he wasn't a cyborg for nothing. All he needed was a little bit of determination, a few more pulls … and the door gave in.

Luckily, the handle didn't break; instead the lock on the inside broke with a loud snap, leaving the entrance useless.

He'd barely broken a sweat as he opened the door and stared at a long staircase leading down.

The seriousness of the situation took over. If he did this, he risked his own life, he risked the Fighters' lives. Just because he'd managed to turn off the cameras didn't mean they'd find out that he was here, and no one would come to save him if everything went south.

Jade was in there.

She'd left him.

Sure, he understood why.

He understood she'd had to go. If she wanted to stay in disguise, she couldn't wait a few more weeks to go back to MedAct. By then it would be too late, but all that didn't justify that *she'd left him*!

Nightmare clenched his teeth.

If he'd just listened to her, they wouldn't be in this situation. They could've come up with a plan to get ahold of the information she was now trying to obtain on her own.

He'd just had to keep telling her no, that he needed her to be safe.

Nightmare shook his head.

Of course, she hadn't listened.

He sighed.

That woman would be the death of him.

Mentally, he prepared himself for whatever was to come, and started to walk down the stairs.

It was time to get this over with.

The long concrete tunnel at the bottom of the stairs was well lit, but it looked nothing like the Fighters' headquarters.

There the walls were white, and everything had a sterile, well-taken-care-of-feeling. Here, the walls were dull, colorless. They made him feel like he really was underground.

He kept his gaze high, focused on what was up ahead. There was nowhere to hide. He could only go forward, and the tunnel seemed to go on forever.

If anything happened, if someone saw him, he could only turn around and run, and hope not to get shot in the back.

After what felt like several agonizing minutes, the tunnel finally came to an end.

Nightmare ended up in front of two double doors with glass windows. He peeked through one window. There was a hallway painted in bright yellow. There were doors on both sides, an elevator with metal doors was nearby, and to the right, he glimpsed stairs just next to where the hallway turned.

Nightmare tried the door handle.

It was open.

Great.

He could continue.

Nightmare went through as quietly as possible, quickly looking around. No one seemed to be aware of his presence. No alarm had gone off yet. Hopefully, he'd managed to sneak in unnoticed, but where should he go to find Jade?

A sign further down the hallway to his right caught his attention. He approached it and read.

Underground floor 4: Archive.

He smiled. *Perfect.* This was where he'd find Jade.

Movement in the corner of his eye caught his attention.

Nightmare turned around.

About twenty feet away, there was a blonde woman wearing a wide smile. It wasn't a nice smile, but the excitement in her brown eyes was unmistakable.

Nightmare tensed, and for a short moment, he could do nothing but stare.

Those eyes …

He *knew* them.

Two huge dark-haired cyborg soldiers stood behind her, and unlike the woman, they weren't smiling. Their gazes were set on him, their hands on their holsters.

Shit!

He whirled around, ready to flee.

Two more cyborg soldiers blocked his way. They towered over him with their seven feet frames, mountains of muscles, and emotionless faces.

Cold chills shot down his spine.

He wasn't small, with his six feet five-inch frame, but the cyborg soldiers made him feel like he was.

They were built for war.

He was built for love.

He was also outnumbered.

Two of them grabbed him and shoved him against the wall.

A short wave of pain surged through his body. He groaned, as dizziness washed over him.

Thankfully, it faded fast and Nightmare grabbed their hands to pull them away, but the cyborg soldiers' grips were like solid rock.

There was no getting away.

The tall woman approached him. She had a masculine appearance, with broad shoulders, strong jawline, and thick eyebrows. She reminded him of someone who'd spent years and years in the military with her straight posture, her hands behind her back, and strong gaze.

He jerked back when she left a feather-light touch on his cheek.

"What a sweet surprise," the woman said, her smile even darker than before. Her eyes were filled with confidence. "I didn't expect to meet you here again ... here where everything started."

Nightmare could only glare, and disbelief filled every part of him. Memories washed over him like a flood of fire, hurting him all over again.

"Have you come back home, Zero? Have you come back so we can continue where we left off?" Her voice was sweet now, way too sweet, with a dark and twisted undertone.

His lower lip trembled. "You can't be—" The words almost didn't come out.

"Can't be what, sweetheart?" She was teasing him.

He shook his head. Sweat broke out on his skin as fear grabbed him, entering his soul. "She's dead. You can't be—"

The woman moved closer, invaded his personal space, as her hand glided over his chest.

The touch made him almost jump out of his own skin. His bond to Jade instantly reacted. It wasn't the slightest pleased with being touched by another woman, a woman he wasn't bound to. The touch was intimate after all, but the pain he'd expected to feel didn't come.

Deep down, he exhaled.

Thank God the damn thing was locked away.

The woman couldn't hurt him.

"And yet, here I am," the woman said. "Say my name. You know me."

Nightmare had never felt this small in his life, as when he stared into the eyes of his creator. "Carolyn."

CHAPTER 27

Jade opened the door to the archive room and peeked inside. The lights were off and the room was silent. She hit the light switch before entering.

Olive giggled behind her and tipped inside the room on her toes. "It almost feels like we're doing something forbidden." She closed the door behind her.

"We are," Jade said and looked around.

That killed her colleague's grin. "We are? I thought you were kidding when you asked me to hack the private server."

"I wasn't."

The room was smaller than her office, and it was windowless. All there was in there was a huge computer, extending from one side of the room to the other. It was about seven feet tall, fifteen feet wide, and as broad as her desk.

Whoever designed it must've had a good taste for delicate

and elegant things. The entire thing was in white, silver, and gray. To reach the hardware, a digital password had to be entered on the glass door to the right, and it would dissolve itself for as long as it was needed.

A lot of fancy blinking was also going on all over it, but the computer didn't make a sound.

Two black screens were attached to it in the middle, and Jade approached one of them. She touched it, and it lit up.

Olive approached with obvious hesitation in her step. "Why exactly do you want me to hack the server? Don't you have access to it?"

"Not everything. Some information, I can only access with the approval of the Council. I've tried to get access to it several times, but they never allowed me to see it. I never understood why until now."

The doctor licked her lips. "Why?"

"Because, if I'm right, MedAct's past is much darker than I thought."

Olive cleared her throat. "I'm not so sure this is a good idea."

Jade pushed a few buttons on the screen. "I could threaten you. I could use your job against you. I could fire you for not helping me."

Her colleague's eyes went wide, and she opened her mouth to speak, but no words came out.

She raised her palm to calm her. "But I'm not going to do that. Instead, I'm going to ask you kindly." She grabbed the woman's hands and looked her deep in the eyes. "Please, help me."

Olive remained still for a long moment. Then she shook her head, and let out a big sigh. "What's going on, Jade?"

"I need someone I can trust. I need someone who has access to this area and who can hack the server, and you're the only one I can trust right now. If I tell you everything that's happened, you'll laugh and think I'm crazy. The only way for me to prove to you something fishy's going on with MedAct is if you hack the server. The proof will be thrown in your face."

She hoped.

The doctor sighed again, but gave her a kind smile. "You have to give me more than that. I'm not going to hack MedAct's private server just because you're MedAct's CEO, and who knows if I'll even be able to get in. Maybe the information you seek is so well guarded it's impossible to reach."

Jade bit her lip. She could only hope that wasn't true, but did she dare reveal more? Would she believe her?

She took a deep breath.

There was only one way to find out.

"I wasn't on vacation."

Olive frowned, then her eyes narrowed. "Then where were you?"

She hesitated, but only for a second. "With the Fighters."

"What?" The question was a yelp-yell.

Jade placed a hand against her lips. "Shh! Someone might hear you. No one can know what we're about to do here."

Olive pulled her hand away. "You were with the Fighters? Are you kidding me?" She seemed more intrigued than angry.

"Nightmare had been shot. They kidnapped me to save his life."

"Oh, wow. I want to hear everything about it."

She nodded. "Fine, but later. Right now, I need you to hack that computer."

Her colleague still didn't move.

Jade cursed silently. It would take years to convince Olive to do what she asked. Her friend was stubborn, but she had one last card to play. "Soul is with them."

A loud gasp went through the room and Olive's eyes went big as bowls. "Is this some kind of sick joke?"

She shook her head. "No, he joined them voluntarily, but I didn't see him when I was there."

"But … how … I mean … why?" The doctor looked ready to cry.

Jade grabbed her hands. "I don't know what happened to him, but don't worry, he's safe and in good hands. The Fighters aren't what we thought they were, but if you want to help Soul, if you want to find out what drove him to do this, you need to help me hack that computer."

Olive sobbed, dried away a tear, nodded, then turned toward the computer. Seconds later, she was pushing digital buttons on one of the screens.

Jade blinked. That had gone unexpectedly easy. She'd expected extended arguing and convincing, but thankfully, it didn't turn out like that.

Time was precious.

Olive remained silent for several minutes, and Jade didn't dare to disturb her. Her concentration was complete.

Occasionally, it seemed like she was having a tough time, other times, she grinned from ear to ear, as if she'd just solved the greatest mystery of life.

"I need your password," the doctor finally said. "It'll make it easier, but there are several passwords I need to figure out for us to access the information."

Jade nodded. "Those are the Council members passwords. Mine is M-E-D, all caps, then eighteen four six hundred twelve."

Olive punched it in. "Thanks." She went quiet again.

Jade returned to watching her. Her colleague sure knew what she was doing. Her fingers worked fast, and with determination. It was amazing how easy she made it look, but it wasn't easy, far from it.

MedAct's defense system was highly evolved and defended. One mistake, and both of them would spend the rest of their lives behind bars. The room would swarm with cyborg soldiers within seconds.

They'd entered this area because both had access. Olive had access because of her technical skills. She not only took care of the cyborg soldiers, she also helped repair computer programs, made sure all servers ran smoothly, and other things Jade barely understood.

Her own expertise was centered in how to create a

cyborg, how to write a cyborg's program, but computer programs were something completely different, because cyborgs weren't computers. They were sentient beings with cybernetic components.

With each passing minute, nerves ratcheted awake within Jade. With every solved password, she came closer and closer to the secrets that'd been kept from her.

"Yes!" Olive announced, after what felt like several hours. She dried the sweat away from her forehead. "I did it. It was a close one, but I did it. It was more difficult than I thought, but this is MedAct we're talking about. I had to go through several defense systems, but thanks to your password, it became easier."

Jade exhaled. "Thank you."

The worst was over.

Her colleague gave a tired smile. "You're welcome." She moved aside.

Jade took Olive's place, and her heart rate shot up. With a shaky hand, she started to look around. The unknown filled her with tension.

She pulled out two portable hard drives no bigger than coins from her pocket, and handed one to Olive. "Transfer everything."

"Got it." The doctor-tech grabbed the device and went to the other screen.

Jade focused on the screen in front of her. Her hands still trembled as she started to look through the files as all information was being downloaded.

Most of the files were logs of progress and tests that'd been performed. Other files shared information about how cyborgs came to be, and how long it took to create them.

Jade scrolled through it all, only noticing a few details here and there. A sentence made her stop.

"Their pointless lives mean nothing to me."

Had Carolyn written that?

Jade kept scrolling. A folder caught her attention.

Zero.

Sweat broke out on her forehead as she clicked it.

Inside were hundreds of other folders, each named with a date. She clicked on the first one, the one with the oldest date.

Inside was a bunch of written information, but also a video. Her hand shook so hard she didn't succeed in opening it until her third attempt.

The video started to play, displaying some kind of old-fashioned infirmary, filled with equipment she didn't recognize, computers with keyboards that were barely used anymore, closets, and a single bed.

Scientists, or doctors, dressed in white robes moved around the bed, some wrote something on papers, others talked.

Then, a woman came into view.

The woman was Carolyn Williams, the creator of MedAct and the cyborgs. Jade recognized her, even if it'd been years since she last saw an image of her.

Carolyn seemed to be in her mid-thirties. She was

attractive, tall, and wore plenty of makeup. Her somewhat frizzy and blonde hair hung loosely down her shoulders as her brown eyes looked straight into the camera.

Her intense determination made Jade go taut, awakening a pinch of insecurity within her. It was an unusual feeling, but the strength this woman radiated was not to play with, and the cold undertone in her expression didn't put Jade at ease.

But also, those eyes seemed awfully familiar. Had she seen them somewhere before?

Carolyn smiled at the camera, but the smile didn't reach her eyes. "Today's a big day. Our first successful cyborg is going to open its eyes for the first time. Our first test subjects never even reached the growth stage, but with Zero, we were able to complete the cycle. It's the world's first cyborg."

Jade cringed.

Carolyn had just called Zero—Nightmare—'*it*'.

Just like in the papers she'd read.

Carolyn grabbed the camera and approached the bed.

Jade gasped. Nightmare lay on it.

A tear ran down her cheek, and her chin started to tremble.

He looked so peaceful, so beautiful. So innocent. Still unaware of all the bad things that were going to happen to him.

Jade wished she could jump through the screen and take him away from it all. She'd never wished for something this badly before.

Olive approached, gasping, too. "Oh my God. Is that—?"

She dried her tears and nodded. "Yes. They're about to wake him up."

Her colleague gave her a look. "Are you crying?"

"Don't worry about it." She focused on the screen.

The two male doctors that stood on the other side of Nightmare's bed looked up at Carolyn.

"Are you sure you want to wake it up?" one of them asked. "We can use its blood, bone marrow, and more without it being conscious."

"I know," Carolyn answered, "but I'm curious."

"What if we can't control it? It's a lot stronger than us."

"Then we'll find a way to control it. Wake it up." She put down the camera on something so that it could easily film the whole scene.

Jade was unable to take her eyes from the screen, as she watched the doctors remove the machine Nightmare was attached to. They injected him with something, and seconds later, he took a big breath, his chest buckled.

Everyone in the room remained still as he started to move.

Eventually, he opened his eyes, and sat, looking around in the room with no expression on his face. There was literally nothing, just dead, cold eyes staring ahead.

Weird.

A newborn cyborg would've been emotional, searching for his bound one, and if he didn't find her, he'd go into panic, but Nightmare was completely still.

Carolyn approached him slowly. "I'm Carolyn Williams. You're creator."

He met her gaze, still without emotions. "My creator."

Both Jade and Olive stared at the screen gaping.

"Did he just speak?" Olive asked.

Jade was unable to confirm out loud. A newborn cyborg couldn't speak. It took a few hours for his mind to start working and processing everything, even language. Everything was about emotions and feelings in the beginning.

"Your name is Zero, and you will do as I say. You belong to me," Carolyn went on.

Nightmare tilted his head.

Was he registering what she was saying? Or was that a hint of dislike in his eyes?

"I belong to you?" he asked.

"Yes. And you will do as I say."

Nightmare remained silent for a while. The dry, emotionless expression on his face made Jade hold her breath. "I will do as you say."

Carolyn grinned. "Good." She reached for the camera. There was a click, and the screen went black.

Jade's heart skipped before settling into a canter. She didn't want to see more, but she had to. She jumped forward, clicking on another folder with a date set several years later.

"I can't believe this. There didn't seem to be a bond," Olive said.

Her gaze jerked to her colleague. "You noticed that, huh?"

The woman frowned. "Of course, I did. He didn't behave like a newborn cyborg."

There was no point in holding anything back anymore. "The bond is the reason I came back, to figure out what Carolyn really meant with it. When I was with the Fighters, they told me the bond is a poison that's programmed to be released into the cyborg's body when his bound one died. At first, I didn't believe it, but I don't doubt it anymore. Now, I have to figure out what the heck is going on."

Olive's eyes were so wide they looked like two spheres. "A poison?" She let out a loud breath. "This is just getting worse and worse."

Jade snorted. "You have no idea." She clicked on another video. "Let's watch this one." It was more difficult to say than she'd expected.

The video started inside an office, with Carolyn in front of it. She looked tired, but also angry. Carolyn glared at the camera and she pulled a hand through her hair. "My curiosity has killed my research. I should've never woken them up. I should've just kept them in a vegetate state and take what I needed to continue my research. Them being awake was never necessary anyway, but I just needed to know, and now look where it has taken us." She let out a long chant of curse words. "They're impossible to control, and if I am going to get what I need for my research, they need to be controlled." She went silent for a while, staring at her desk, before looking into the camera again. "The problem is, I need many of them. A few cyborgs won't fuel my research, and I need to find a way to make that happen. I won't let anything stand in my way." Carolyn leaned closer to the camera. "I have a plan. It's still in construction mode, but if it works, it will change everything." She grinned. "I call it 'the bond,' and I intend to use it on Zero, if he ever fails me again." The screen went black.

Jade didn't move. For a long moment, she was barely able to breathe. "The cyborgs were meant for something else. She didn't create them to help lonely women. She created them for something else."

Olive didn't move, either. She seemed just as flabbergasted. "Well, this turned out to be a life-changing day."

A click sounded from both screens.

"The information has been transferred," Olive said and gave both hard drives to Jade.

She stared at them. Right now, she held the most precious thing in the whole world. All the answers the Fighters ever needed were on these two drives.

And she was going to give them to the Fighters.

Jade placed them inside an inner pocket of her jeans and closed it, knowing they'd be safe there.

The other screen beeped.

Olive approached to check what was going on. A frown grew on her forehead. "The cameras outside, near the emergency exit, have been turned off."

"What?" Jade was instantly by her side, watching the screen.

"Something from the outside hacked the system and turned them off."

"When?"

She pushed a few buttons. "About twenty minutes ago. The defense system was tricked into thinking it was an authorized move, but it discovered just now that it was not the case."

Jade frowned. "What do you mean it was tricked? It's a fool-proof system."

"And yet, it was hacked." Olive pushed a few more buttons.

A few more seconds passed with Jade trying to calculate what could've happened, then it hit her, and she gasped. "Nightmare."

Had he really followed her? Was he that stupid?

She had to know. "Quickly. Check the cameras nearest the emergency exit."

Olive did as she asked. "The ones on the inside are still on."

Thank God.

That would make it easier to find him, if it was him, but who else could it be?

"Show me every camera on the lower floor."

Her colleague clicked a few things, and five images showed up on the screen, showing different parts of the lower floor.

Some cameras showed parts of a hallway, one was pointed toward a door, and the third one …

"Oh, my god!" Jade almost screamed.

Nightmare was held against the wall by two cyborg

soldiers in the middle of a hallway.

Two others stood nearby, and Soul's bound one, Janice Walker stood in front of Nightmare with a wide grin, as she talked to him.

Jade's lower lip trembled.

He'd been beaten.

The way he leaned forward, the pain written on his face, the bloodied lip, and the red eye spoke no other language.

"Turn on the sound!" she yelled to Olive.

What the heck was Janice doing?

The doctor-tech pushed a button.

"Have you missed me, Zero?" Janice asked with a sweet, but cold smile and caressed Nightmare's cheek.

Jade's blood started to boil.

How dared she?

Nightmare glared with pure fury, hate, and disgust at Janice. "Don't imagine anything, Carolyn. You mean nothing to me, and you never have."

What?

Had he just called Janice *Carolyn*?

Was he malfunctioning?

Janice looked nothing like the Carolyn she'd just seen in the videos.

Janice had a more masculine appearance, with a fit and tall body, and Carolyn was more feminine-looking, with a styled and attractive appearance.

"Aww, isn't that a shame." The woman's grin didn't fade, but her sweet voice pissed Jade off, even more so when she placed her hand on Nightmare's chest. "But I'm sure your bond has." She met his gaze.

Nightmare flattened his lips, obviously refusing to answer.

"What is this?" Olive asked, the confusion in her voice was clear.

"I don't know," Jade said with barely a whisper, but something was very, *very* wrong.

"You and I used to have so much fun together," Janice told Nightmare. "I'm sure we can have fun again. What do you think of that? You're in my arms again."

"You'll never have control over me again," her cyborg hissed and pulled on his arms in an attempt to get free, but the soldiers didn't budge. "But I would love to know how come you're alive. Your eyes are the same, but you look different."

Janice chuckled. "It's all thanks to you, your since long dead brothers, and many other cyborgs. You all were never anything but toys to fulfill a greater purpose. Your lives mean nothing. You were created for one reason only, and I will make sure you all fulfill that purpose."

Jade's anger boiled over. "That's it! I've heard enough." She grabbed the gun she'd taken from her office, and headed for the door.

Olive grabbed her arms. "Wait! You can't be serious about going out there."

"I have to. There's no other way." She pulled out one of the hard drives from her inner pocket and handed it to

257

Olive. "Keep this safe. Stay here, and don't let them see you. Leave once it's safe. I need to get him out of here. I'll be in touch."

Confusion was written all over her colleague's expression, but she took the hard drive. "I have no idea what's going on, but something is messed up for sure." Determination awakened in her eyes. "You can count on me, but you'll put yourself in danger going out there."

She took a deep breath. "I need to help him."

"Why?"

"Because I'm his bound one." She exited the room, leaving a gaping Olive behind.

CHAPTER 28

Nightmare stared at the woman in front of him. She reminded him of Carolyn, but at the same time, she didn't. Her hair was blonde, but darker. Her eyes were brown, but brighter. The shape of her head was different, more prominent.

She was like a subtle imposter of the Carolyn he'd once known; gentle changes here and there, but still enough for her to look like a long distant relative.

This Carolyn looked physically stronger, fiercer, than the elegant and feminine Carolyn from his past.

Yet, she *was* Carolyn.

The disbelief was overwhelming, but he didn't doubt it. It *was* her.

How?

And why did she look so young?

She seemed to be in her forties, but Carolyn *died* about

forty years ago. He hadn't seen it, but he'd heard about it.

It'd been all over the news, and he'd almost died with her, when his bond had gone crazy. He'd learned then how dangerous the bond really was.

She'd never told him about the poison, but he'd figured it out.

The first few weeks after her death had been hell. His bond had started screaming after a new bound one once it realized it couldn't kill him.

Every day had been a struggle to not go after the first woman he saw. Somehow, Nightmare had managed to stay hidden and put his signal together, the signal that blocked the bond.

He'd managed to place it inside himself and put the bond away for good. Only, the need for another bound one remained. Ever since that day, it'd been like an addiction he hadn't been able to shake.

But now, another bond lived in his heart.

His bond to Jade.

A bond that *didn't* control him.

The thought of her filled him will love and a pinch of joy, despite the situation. The image of her beautiful face, her dark eyes, golden skin, made his lips twitch. He'd fallen in love with her on his own *before* the bond had been initiated, and it warmed his heart.

He loved her.

He *really* did.

How he wished he'd told her. Now, it looked like he'd

never be able to.

Carolyn moved even closer. "You're smiling. Your bond remembers me, doesn't it?" Her hand glided down his chest.

Nightmare frowned. Did she think his bond for her was still active?

He snorted internally. Of *course,* she did.

She knew nothing about the progress he'd achieved these past forty years. All she knew was that he was a dirty, dangerous, and untrustworthy Fighter who struggled in life. Carolyn only knew what the media shared.

In other words, *nothing.*

He could use this.

"Yes, it remembers." It was almost impossible to speak the lie, especially with that pinch of longing he added to his voice.

"Good. Then it will remember this too." She leaned in for a kiss.

Nightmare inhaled sharply. His bond to Jade started to scratch on his insides as she moved closer.

Thank God that awful thing was locked away but Carolyn couldn't find out about it. If she discovered he was bound to someone else, things would take an ugly turn.

Carolyn aimed for his lips.

Despair washed over him, but all he could do was allow it to happen.

"Get away from him!"

He winced from the sudden voice filling the hallway. Nightmare turned his head.

Jade stood a few feet away, with a gun pointed straight at them. Her hand trembled but the determination in her narrowed gaze was obvious.

All eyes were suddenly on her.

"Jade," he whispered, unable to hold back a smile. He'd never been so happy to see her, but she shouldn't be here.

She should run; he needed her safe, but he was too tired, to achy all over from the beating to tell her that.

Carolyn gave him a side-glare.

Nightmare flattened his lips. Had she noticed the love in his voice?

Carolyn's focus returned to Jade. She smiled. "Jade. What're you doing here? I thought you were on vacation."

"I just came back." His bound one's voice was cold. "Release him."

His former bound one frowned. "Release him? You must've forgotten what we do with the Fighters here. Besides, he walked in here of his own free will. I'm just making sure he doesn't do anything stupid."

"By beating him up? Last time I checked, we don't hurt the Fighters."

Carolyn hesitated. "He was resisting. I had to calm him down."

Jade snorted and glared. Pure hatred shone in her eyes. She'd stormed right in with the gun ready. She hadn't been taken by surprise.

That could only mean one thing.

Jade knew.

Nightmare raised his head, and instantly found the camera on the ceiling a few feet away. His lips twitched as pride filled him.

Fear lingered in the back of her gaze, but she didn't allow it to rule. "Don't take me for a fool," Jade hissed. "I heard everything—Carolyn." She spit out the name. "Now let him go, or I'll put a bullet through your head."

The woman's jaw dropped. Then she found the camera as well. "I see. I guess that means the game is over." With what seemed like lightning speed, she pulled out a small gun from a back pocket and pointed it straight at Nightmare's forehead.

He winced. How had she managed to pull out the gun that fast?

He barely got the chance to blink before it was in her hand. Not even a cyborg was that fast, but then again, she should be dead. Somehow, she'd stopped herself from aging and even changed her appearance.

The cyborg soldiers didn't move, but they studied the situation.

"I suggest you put away your gun," Carolyn said. "You wouldn't want Zero to get hurt, now would you?"

"His name is Nightmare, and if you hurt him, you'll be dead before you reach the floor."

His heart stirred. This was definitely not the right situation to be overcome by sweet and lovey-dovey emotions, but he couldn't help it. Everything she was doing right now intensified his love for her.

Jade shook her head, and disbelief filled her expression. "I can't believe this. You and I have worked together for years. Not even once did it occur to me that you're Carolyn. How's it even possible?"

Her eyes were filled with dark amusement. "Do you really believe I'd walk away so easily from my life's work?"

"But you died."

She nodded. "Yes, I did. I got hit by a car. I never thought it'd end like that. I was too consumed by my own thoughts and I didn't watch where I was going. Just like that, it was all over. I woke up days later. My doctors brought me back, but by then, the world had already been told I was dead. I decided to use that."

"And how have you been able to stay this young? And what about Soul?"

Carolyn grinned. "Soul was nothing more but a tool, and when it comes to my youth, I'm sorry, but I won't share my masterpiece with you. Let's focus on more important things, shall we?" She pressed the gun against Nightmare's forehead. "Like, how're you going to get out of this situation, without getting both of you killed?"

"That's easy. You've obviously forgotten who I am," Jade said. Her gaze shot to the two cyborg soldiers that held Nightmare in place. "By my authority as MedAct's CEO, I order you to release him."

Silence filled the area for two seconds.

Then the two cyborg soldiers reacted.

They moved, backing fast, forcing a surprised Carolyn to

move away with them.

"Take the gun and keep her away from us. Protect us," Jade told the cyborg soldiers.

One of them instantly lunged at Carolyn. He grabbed her hand and pulled the gun from her grip while the other three blocked her way to Jade and Nightmare.

The woman cursed, and a strong fight lit up in her eyes. "What the heck do you think you're doing?" She glared at the cyborg soldiers, but they ignored her. She couldn't hurt them.

Nightmare fell to the floor with a loud groan. His body hurt, every muscle ached.

Jade was instantly by his side.

He gave her a tired smile, still happy to see her.

"I'll never forgive you for following me," she whispered with a glare.

He only chuckled. "I'll kiss your anger away until you forgive me," he whispered back.

She rolled her eyes and helped him stand.

Pain surged through him. Even if he loved her touch, it hurt having her hands on his tender limbs. Hopefully, he wasn't bleeding internally, but the cyborg soldiers had beaten him effectively. Every muscle ached, his face felt swollen, and the taste of blood was in his mouth.

Jade turned to them with his arm wrapped around her shoulder. "I'm sure you've noticed Soul isn't here anymore. You'll soon realize why. Once you do, come find us."

They walked away.

Nightmare groaned. The pain was like a knife in his chest with every step he took, but no way in hell was he staying here just because it hurt.

"You idiots!" Carolyn roared and tried to push through the cyborg soldiers. "Get out of my way, you big buffoons!"

Nightmare only grinned when one of the soldiers lifted his arm in front of Carolyn and pushed her back.

The cyborg didn't even look at her. His gaze was fixed at them.

So were the other soldiers' gazes.

There was something in their eyes. Was it … sadness?

It was hard to tell. It was too invisible, but they knew something was going on. Watching their CEO help the enemy had to be a sight, and yet, they didn't disobey Jade.

"You can't walk away from me, Zero!" Carolyn yelled. "You're bound to me. Your heart will always come back to me."

Nightmare froze, and for a short moment, he stared ahead.

Jade grabbed the hand he held over her shoulder and gently squeezed it.

That tiny gesture made him feel her support, and he badly needed it right now.

Then he whirled around. Pure hatred, disgust, and fury filled every part of his body as he pierced his creator with his glare.

The vile woman twitched and silenced.

Her reaction felt like a small victory, because he didn't

miss the sudden surprise and fear in her eyes.

"The next time we meet will be the time I kill you. Remember that," Nightmare vowed. He continued walking away with his *true* bound one by his side, not bothering with giving Carolyn a final look.

CHAPTER 29

Jade didn't speak as Nightmare guided her to where he'd entered MedAct. She was too angry to open her mouth. Too many harsh words would come out if she tried. Keeping them in was for the best ... for now.

Besides, he needed her right now. He was able to walk, but he was leaning forward with agony in his expression. Sweat covered his forehead, and he was shaking in obvious pain.

He let out a groan but didn't protest.

They kept walking.

She had to examine him, but Jade didn't dare to stop, and neither did he try. His gaze was focused up ahead.

The long concrete tunnel seemed to go on forever, but eventually, they reached a metal door.

She opened it and helped him out. The lock was broken, and it didn't take much to figure out how he'd gotten in.

Jade looked around. They were behind the MedAct building, in an open and empty area. There was a motorcycle not far. She led him to it. "I'll drive." She grabbed the helmet and handed it to him.

Nightmare frowned.

"There's only one. Take it," she said, pushing it to him.

"You're more fragile. You should have it."

She narrowed her eyes. "You're the one who's hurt."

He pressed his lips together. "Stop arguing, woman, and put it on. We don't have time for this." Her cyborg groaned again, and pain marked his face. Nightmare placed his hand against his chest.

He was right. Arguing was a bad idea.

Jade put the helmet on his head.

"What the—?" He reached for it.

"Don't you dare," she hissed. "Do you want people to recognize you?"

He stilled.

"I didn't think so," she went on as she sat at the front of the motorcycle. "Now, get on. As you said, we don't have time for this."

Nightmare let out a long chant of curse words, but sat behind her, wrapping his arms around her waist with another grunt of discomfort.

She flinched on the inside, almost feeling his pain as her own. She really had to take a look at him, fast.

He could be bleeding internally.

Jade started the motorcycle, and they were off.

They rode through the city in silence.

It would've been impossible to talk anyway, because of the wind ruffling her hair and singing in her ears. With each mile, the tension in her body started to lessen.

They'd be safe soon.

Just a little bit longer and they'd be back at the Fighters' headquarters. She'd be able to take care of her cyborg then.

When they'd finally left the city behind, and entered the countryside, she relaxed. MedAct was far behind, and no one seemed to be following them.

They cyborg soldiers seemed to have understood something was off and had followed her orders. They'd helped. They'd saved them, actually.

They were programmed to follow orders. It was an instinct, almost impossible to ignore, and yet, Soul had ignored it.

Maybe these cyborg soldiers would be able to do that too, but would they be able to leave their bound ones?

Jade bit her lip.

Poor Soul.

What he must've gone through. She understood him better now. He must've figured everything out. Maybe he even knew Janice was Carolyn.

She'd seen him flinch whenever Janice's name had been mentioned, but she'd never reflected over it. Cyborgs weren't meant to dislike their bound ones.

They're supposed to love them, and yet, Soul hadn't.

Anger boiled her veins.

What had Janice—no, Carolyn—done to the poor cyborg?

She'd make her regret hurting him.

Determination stirred within Jade. Something told her Soul wasn't at the Fighters' headquarters after all. He wasn't locked up like some of the Fighters.

No, he was out there somewhere, hiding.

She'd make sure he got the help he needed and help bring him home.

To the Fighters.

Home.

Jade smirked.

It was her home now, too. MedAct wasn't her place anymore.

She'd never be able to go back after what just happened. Who knew what Carolyn would do now, but one thing she was sure of.

The evil woman would go to the Council and tell them about Jade's betrayal.

She inhaled despite the moving air kissing her cheeks.

She was no longer the CEO of MedAct, and soon, it would be official. Her betrayal would be announced to the world, and people would start believing lies about her, without ever knowing the real story.

There had to be a way to change that.

MedAct was the bad guy, not the Fighters, like most of the world believed.

Jade didn't want to imagine what Nightmare had gone

through all these years. The truth had been in his hands, but no one had ever listened.

Including her.

In a way, she could put herself in his shoes.

She understood now.

Nightmare pulled at her shirt.

Her attention shot to him. Was something wrong?

His head rested heavily against her back and his arms barely gripped her.

Luckily, the city was far behind them, and they'd just entered the forest.

She found a side road and drove in between the trees. Jade stopped and dismounted the motorcycle.

Nightmare listed forward on the seat, swaying, and his head dangling. He started to slide off.

She grabbed him, her stomach clenching. She held on all she could, but it was pointless.

He was too heavy.

Nightmare landed on the grass on his back. He groaned and remained still.

Jade didn't hesitate. She took off the helmet and tossed it over her shoulder.

He panted as she opened his shirt.

She studied his torso. Usually, she would've enjoyed the sights of his muscular body, but all those dark bruises made her heart stutter, and her fury spiked.

The cyborg soldiers were strong, and this was all Carolyn's doing.

She'd be the one to pay for this.

Nightmare didn't move, but he watched her when she pulled her phone out and dialed a number.

"Hello? Jade?" Celise's worried voice was loud on the other side of the line.

"Celise. Yes, it's me. Nightmare's hurt. I need your help. I need you to grab a few Fighters and pick us up. We're in the middle of the forest, and I can't move him. It's too far for him to travel on the motorcycle. I think he's got a broken rib."

"Oh, my God! We're on the way."

The line went dead.

Jade frowned. "I didn't get to tell her our location."

Nightmare's lips twitched. "Don't worry. She'll find us."

Her frown deepened. "How?"

"Celise invented a program to track down cyborgs through the universal signal that unites us all. That's how she managed to find Shade several weeks ago. We all felt her use it." He gasped suddenly, as if surprised, then he relaxed and smiled. "She's at it right now. I feel it working."

Her jaw dropped. "I didn't know."

He grabbed her hand, gently squeezed it. "You know now."

She looked away. "I'll never be able to go back."

A part of her mourned what she'd lost, but another part was happy that her eyes had been opened.

Nightmare's grasp on her hand tightened. "You'll be MedAct's CEO one day again. I promise you. Once we've cleaned up this mess, we'll turn MedAct into what it is meant to be—a haven for cyborgs."

"That's wishful thinking. Janice …" She swallowed hard. "Carolyn … will try to take control now, and she'll succeed when she tells everyone I've changed sides." Jade shook her head. "I still can't grasp that … I mean, she's alive, and …" The words died when she met her cyborg's gaze.

He didn't move, only studied her with expressionless eyes. "When I realized who she was, I thought my whole world would collapse again," Nightmare finally said. "I felt fear and hatred, but after a while … I felt a slight relief."

Jade winced. "Relief?"

That was the last thing she'd expected him to say.

"Revenge slipped by me about forty years ago. I was furious at her for getting killed so easily, for getting killed by something else than my hands. I won't fail this time. Besides, Carolyn still believes I'm bound to her. I intend to use that."

Had she heard him right?

Why wasn't he in shock?

Why didn't the knowledge Carolyn was alive scare him?

Carolyn being alive was disturbing to say in the least, but Nightmare was full of determination, a determination so strong it was almost overwhelming.

Funny, but seeing him like this, calmed her too.

"This time, my face will be the last thing she sees as she takes her final breath," Nightmare's dark vow was present in every word.

Jade didn't object.

After what Carolyn had done, she deserved no mercy.

Especially not now, since she'd been hiding in plain sight. Only God knew what she'd done behind Jade's back.

The thought sent daggers down her spine.

She barely dared to imagine what the vile woman was planning, but from what she'd learned these last few days, it would be far from good.

Jade squeezed Nightmare's hand and gave him a smile. "And I will stand by your side through it all."

He smiled back.

The resolve in his eyes faded and made room for sweet emotions. The love and desire in their shining depths made her look away. She cleared her throat and her cheeks heated. "Why're you looking at me like that?"

"Because I love you."

She stilled. Unwelcome heaviness settled in her chest. Words she'd always wanted to hear. But they weren't real. "That's the bond talking." Disappointment made her want to close her eyes.

"No, it's not."

Jade blinked. "It's not?"

"I'm sure you've wondered why my bond to *you* got sealed away without reason, and why my eyes flashed without you even touching me. I'm sure you can figure it out, if you just give it a thought."

Nightmare looked so tired. He had to be in a lot of pain, but there was nothing she could do for him.

Jade had no medical equipment, but nothing pointed her to believe he was bleeding internally. All she could do was keep him company.

His gaze never left her, as she sat by his side and held his hand in hers.

It was almost as if he was expecting something from her.

Jade licked her lips. A pinch of excitement filled her.

He seemed willing to reveal whatever he'd been hiding these last few days.

"Is it because of your old bond?"

Nightmare shook his head with an amused grin.

"Is it because the new bond malfunctioned somehow?" Her cheeks became even warmer when the love in his eyes intensified.

He looked at her as if he'd never seen anything more beautiful, as if she was a part of his soul.

Her cyborg caressed the back of her hand with his thumb and gave her the sweetest smile. "It's because I fell in love with you."

Silence fell between them.

The wind blew, and birds sang in the distance, but Jade barely noticed. "You mean … the bond made you fall in love with me?" He couldn't possibly mean that literally, right?

Nightmare's smile widened. "No, because I fell in love with you a long time ago on my own, and the bond got locked away … because my heart was already filled with you. That's also why it didn't need me to touch you to initiate. It just waited for the right moment, the moment when you told me you loved me."

Her jaw dropped. Her heart took off, rebounding off her ribs.

"I've never known love. Not *true* love," he said. "I didn't understand it, and because of that, I didn't understand my feelings for you until the bond initiated, instead, I pushed them aside. I ignored them. The love I had for Carolyn was not by my own choice. I hated every second of it, but this is *different*. This love I choose to embrace, because my heart chose it itself."

A tear ran down her cheek and she swiped it away. "I don't know what to say." She giggled, couldn't help it.

He grinned. "Just tell me you love me."

She laughed again. It was delighted, even to her ears. "I do. I really do. I love you."

Nightmare pulled her over him.

She threw out her hands and stopped herself from falling over his bruised chest. Jade peered into his shining eyes. "I could've hurt you."

"But you didn't. Now, shut up and kiss me."

That was a command she couldn't resist.

CHAPTER 30

Jade stared at the little hard drive in her shaky palm. She hadn't been this nervous in a long time.

This was the day that was about to change everything.

Everything.

The empty gathering room was huge, but soon, it would be filled with Fighters. Fighters that wanted to know what'd happened.

Nightmare's arms wrapped around her from behind, and she leaned into his embrace.

It was comforting, filled with love, and support. She could rely on him.

He'd be there for her, and testify to her story, as she'd testify to his.

The Fighters still didn't completely trust her, even if she'd come back with more than they could've ever asked for.

That would hopefully change soon, because soon, they'd

know what they were up against.

Soon, they'd known how much had been hidden behind their backs.

Telling them Carolyn was alive would be difficult.

They hadn't waited long yesterday in the forest for the Fighters to arrive.

Celise and Wind had been with them, but because of Nightmare's condition, few questions had been answered. The leader had been taken to the infirmary and she'd helped him heal.

Now, they were inside the gathering room, waiting for everyone to arrive.

This was going to be the most difficult talk Jade had ever had.

Nightmare gently kissed her head. "I'm right here, by your side. We'll do this together."

She nodded and caressed his arm. Feeling the heat of his skin against her palm calmed her. "You should be the train-wreck, not me."

"I know. It's strange, but I'm not. Knowing she's alive gives me some kind of weird inner peace. Now, I can finally get my revenge."

Jade wouldn't stop him. The betrayal *she* felt was nothing compared to his.

Finding out Carolyn had been disguised as Janice, hit her hard. She still felt the effect from the shock and the surprise. It was unbelievable.

She'd studied Nightmare from the moment they'd come

back. Expecting some kind of denial or negative reaction, but instead, she'd seen pure fortitude. There never was any fear or shock.

Just that pure determination.

Nightmare had a new goal now.

She just hoped it wouldn't ruin them all.

Cyborgs and humans started to enter the gathering room.

No one said anything, but they all looked at her and Nightmare.

What they thought, she couldn't tell, but some seemed to be expecting the worst.

Jade didn't blame them.

"What happened yesterday?" Blaze was the first to speak, once everyone was seated. Attention in the room was rapt.

Jade gave Nightmare a quick look, looking for some support, and the smile she got filled her with strength.

She took a step forward, displaying the hard drive in her hand. "This is the answer to all our questions."

Murmurs went through the room and over twenty pairs of wide eyes stared at *her*.

"I managed to access the private server and withdraw the information. I only got a quick glance at it before I had to leave, but what I saw … it was—" Jade clenched her jaw.

The disappointment still sang in her heart. She'd always been proud of MedAct, loved working and being a part of the company. It'd been a dream, but that dream was now shattered. Her gaze landed on Celise. "I understand now, and I'm sorry for ever mistrusting you."

Her colleague gave a sharp nod and smiled.

"MedAct is hiding more than I ever imagined. The council always told me there was nothing of interest on the private server, and I trusted them," Jade went on. "I don't know what they're hiding but what I do know is Carolyn had other plans for the cyborgs than becoming a woman's true love."

"What do you mean?" Silver asked, his expression was harsh, but his hold on his bound one was gentle.

Faye held him just as tightly.

"We need to study the information on the hard drive."

"I can't believe it," someone said from the back.

Many shook their heads and just as many eyes were filled with disbelief.

"There's something else," Nightmare said and stood next to Jade, taking her hand in his.

She tensed. Knew what he was about to say, and *he* had to be the one to say it.

"Carolyn's alive." His voice was loud and clear.

It was as if death itself had suddenly walked into the room. All the color drained from everyone's faces.

The air grew thick, so thick it was difficult to breathe. Many jaws hung low, and no one said anything. No one seemed able to.

They were waiting for more.

"I managed to sneak into MedAct in my attempt to find Jade," Nightmare continued with no emotions on his face.

"But before I got anywhere, I was surrounded by cyborg soldiers and Carolyn. I recognized her, but her appearance was different. It was definitely her … and she was young."

Silver flew up. "Is this a joke?"

Faye, who sat next to him, had her hands over her mouth. Her wide eyes were filled with tears and shock.

The leader shook his head and took a deep breath. A pinch of sadness reflected in his shining eyes. His hands trembled, but he seemed to recover fast.

Deep down, Jade hoped he'd allow himself to feel, to let go.

He needed to process the situation, but chose instead to suck it up. This inkling of emotion was proof enough he wasn't as strong on the inside as she'd first thought.

"It's no joke," she said because Nightmare seemed unable to say anything else. He was trying to keep it together. "And not only that, she's been hiding in plain sight as Janice Walker, Soul's bound one."

Celise flew up from her chair. "What!"

Jade's heart clenched. Poor Soul. She barely dared to imagine what he'd gone through. What if Carolyn had treated him the same way she'd treated Nightmare? Only, he'd never told anyone anything.

Tears gathered in Celise's eyes. She opened her mouth but was unable to speak.

"Janice … Carolyn … said she died but was brought back. She refused to answer why she looked so young." She gazed at the precious hard drive in her hand before looking at the Fighters again.

Their expressions were still the same, if not more intense. Everyone wanted answers.

Everyone wanted to know what the hell was going on.

This was beyond what everyone had ever imagined.

"I have no answers now, but believe me, we'll do everything in our power to find out what's going on." A tear ran down Jade's cheek and she quickly wiped it away. "From this day on, I am no longer the CEO of MedAct. Carolyn will make sure of that. All I'm asking of you is to trust me." She raised her hand with the device. "This hard drive is yours now." She handed it to her cyborg.

They exchanged a quick look.

Nightmare gave her a gentle and comforting smile.

For a long moment, no one moved.

Her hope sank. Was this still not enough to convince them she wasn't the bad guy?

Would they never give her a chance?

Phoenix stood and approached. "I must say I had my doubts. I wasn't completely sure if releasing you was the right thing to do, but now I know it was. You have my trust. With you among us, I'm sure we'll be able to achieve everything we ever hoped for."

A small part of her rejoiced. "Thank you."

All around the room, one smile after another appeared. The Fighters nodded, giving their approval, and Jade smiled back, meeting each one of their gazes.

It felt good.

Her relationship with them would turn out all right after all.

Phoenix turned to Nightmare. "What about Soul? He's going to need our help. We need to find him."

Her shoulders tightened again. "He isn't here, is he?"

Silver approached. "Soul went into hiding. He chose not to stay with us, because of the tracking device that's implanted within him."

That didn't sound good.

"We need to find him. He needs to know what's going on. I've no idea if he even knows his bound one is Carolyn." A shiver went through her. Saying it out loud made it somehow more real.

Nightmare squeezed her hand. "He'll contact us when the time comes."

CHAPTER 31

Jade sat on the edge of the bed and watched her cyborg undress. She smirked when she saw his eagerness and desire, but when his shirt dropped to the floor and the dark bruises on his chest filled her sight, her smile faded.

Nightmare knelt in front of her. "Why the sudden sad face?"

She took a deep breath. "Everything rushed back to me." Even if she hadn't witnessed the abuse, she kept seeing it in front of her, how the cyborg soldiers beat Nightmare on Carolyn's order.

They'd spent hours in the gathering room together with the Fighters, and the others, explaining everything. What'd surprised people the most, besides Carolyn being alive, was that the evil woman still thought Nightmare was bound to her. Yet, she'd tortured him. That said a lot about what a cold bitch she was.

He gently caressed her cheek. "Don't let it set. Despite everything that's happened, we're both safe."

Jade snorted. "I'm still angry at you for following me."

"And I'm angry at you for leaving." He didn't look the slightest bit upset though, just amused.

"There was no other way."

"I know." Nightmare grabbed her shirt and took it off. "Now, let's talk about more important things, like when we're getting married, and how many children we're going to have," he said as he lay her down on the bed and hovered over her.

She gaped. "Are you serious?"

He chuckled and kissed her cheek. "I've never been more serious. Despite the situation we're in, I've never been this happy in my whole life. I'm not alone anymore, the bond doesn't rule me, and my feelings for you are true; they are my own. You've no idea how good that feels." Her cyborg kissed her other cheek, and his fingertips slid down her arms, awakening goosebumps on her skin. "I want to spend every day of my life by your side. For so many years, I was afraid to belong to a woman again, but not anymore." His lips grazed her throat. "You have my heart ... forever."

Jade trembled. His gentle touches and kisses ignited her from the inside out, making her long for more.

She'd never dared to think about marriage and children. It'd never even crossed her mind, but now, it was almost thrilling. "This isn't a good time to have children."

He met her gaze. "True, but the fight with MedAct won't

go on forever."

Jade swallowed; her blood pressure rose. "I'm not that young anymore either."

"You're in your late thirties. You still have some time." He leaned closer to her ear and whispered. "I know you want this. Say yes."

She gulped. "Marriage? Children?"

"Is it that bad? The marriage-part we can do right away."

She stared at the ceiling, as he kept teasing her with his lips.

His hands trailed down her body, slowly undressing her.

Jade hadn't seen this coming. She'd never seen him like the type who would want to marry and start a family. "Have you thought much about it?"

"I just started." He dropped her pants on the floor. "We have a long and difficult road ahead of us. Not just you and me, but every Fighter. Celise, Faye, and Wind, as well. Despite all the difficulties it'll bring, I intend to be happy with you in the middle of it all." A small grin decorated his luscious mouth. "So, Jade, will you marry me?" His shining gaze was filled with hope and anticipation.

She could finally have everything she'd ever dreamt of; everything she'd denied herself.

Nightmare was hers, and she was his.

They belonged together.

Not because of the bond, but because of love, *true* love.

She'd do anything for him, and he'd do anything for her. It was obvious in his love-filled expression.

They were a perfect match.

Jade smiled and caressed his cheek. Her feelings for him filled her heart. "Yes."

A gentle flash sparked in Nightmare's eyes. "Tomorrow. I will not wait a day longer."

"And where are you going to find a priest by tomorrow?"

He smirked. "I'll ask Blue."

Jade blinked. "He used to be a priest?"

Nightmare nodded. "It wasn't put into his programming, but he became interested in the profession and decided to go for it. Unfortunately, Blue didn't get the chance to work as one. He'd just finished his education when his bound one died."

"I guess we can't let his skills go to waste then."

He grinned. "No, we can't."

Jade grinned back and caressed his cheek again. "Tomorrow it is."

THANK YOU

Thank you for reading my story. I hope you enjoyed it.
You can soon look forward to book five the the Bound by
Her series - *Shattared Cyborg*. Soul's and Olive's story.

PREVIOUS BOOKS IN THE SERIES:

Her Cyborg - Book 1

Tempted Cyborg - Book 1.5

Loved Cyborg - Book 2

Kissed Cyborg - Book 3

ABOUT THE AUTHOR

Nellie C. Lind lives in Sweden with her son, but she was born in Poland. Writing has always been one of her greatest interests. Today, she runs the publishing house, Sense of Romance.

She writes passionate paranormal romance, fantasy, and science fiction books for adult readers. You'll find all sorts of beings in her stories, such as angels, vampires, gods, and elves.

You'll also find everything from short stories to novels among her books. Keep an eye open for upcoming releases!

Website: nellieclind.com
Blog: sense-of-romance.com

www.ingramcontent.com/pod-product-compliance
Lightning Source LLC
Chambersburg PA
CBHW061946170626
46813CB00006B/2547